The Scent of Fear

Margaret Yorke

COMPASS PRESS

* OXFORD * MELBOURNE *

Copyright © Margaret Yorke 1980

First published in 1980 by Hutchinson & Co (Publishers) Ltd

Compass Press Large Print Book Series; an imprint of
ISIS Publishing Ltd, Great Britain, and Bolinda Press, Australia
Published in Large Print 2000 by ISIS Publishing Ltd,
7 Centremead, Osney Mead, Oxford OX2 0ES,
and Bolinda Publishing Pty Ltd,
17 Mohr Street, Tullamarine, Victoria 3043
by arrangement with Curtis Brown

**British Library Cataloguing
in Publication Data**
  Yorke, Margaret
  The scent of fear. – Large
  print ed.
  1. Dectective and mystery stories
  2. Large type books
I. Title
823.9′14 [F]

**Australian Cataloguing in
Publication Data**
  Yorke, Margaret
  The scent of fear/
  Margaret Yorke
  1. Large print books.
  2. Detective and mystery stories,
  English.
  I. Title.
  823.914

ISBN 0-7531-6159-1 (hb) 0-7531-6266-0 (pb)
(ISIS Publishing Ltd)
ISBN 1-74030-239-7 (hb) 1-74030-240-0 (pb)
(Bolinda Publishing Pty Ltd)

Printed and bound by Antony Rowe, Chippenham and Reading

To Patty, with love

All the characters and events in this story are imaginary.
Any resemblance to real places or people is coincidence.

CHAPTER
ONE

It was still dark.

Mrs Anderson reached for the lamp. Searching for the switch, her fumbling fingers met the tumbler of water on the bedside table and knocked it over. When she turned on the light, water was dripping on to her library book, the eiderdown, and the worn carpet. Stiffly, the old lady pushed herself round so that she sat on the side of the bed. Her feet groped their way into the slippers left nearby as she pulled the faded blue wool dressing-gown, which lay at the end of the bed, round her thin shoulders, sliding her arms into the sleeves. She struggled up, opened her bedroom door and shuffled along the passage to the bathroom.

The figure descending the staircase from the top floor of the big old house froze when the shaft of light spread across the landing. He waited until he heard the plug pull and Mrs Anderson's slow progress back to her room. As soon as her door closed he slipped quietly along the passage, down the main staircase and out through the dining-room window, the way he always came and went.

Looking back at the house, he could see that Mrs Anderson's light was still on. She often woke at night.

He'd sometimes wondered how she'd react if he suddenly appeared in her bedroom. Drop dead, maybe. He might try it, some night. He ran across the garden and along the drive to the gate, where his motor-bike was hidden in the bushes. Straddling it, he freewheeled down the hill towards the by-pass, starting the engine only when he reached the bottom: not that there was anyone to hear him — the old woman wouldn't and there were no other houses near.

In her bedroom, Mrs Anderson put on the electric kettle she kept there, together with teabags and a cup and saucer; she took up a small jug of milk each night at bedtime. A cup of tea in the night was a comfort when she could not sleep. Tonight, she had brought a towel with her when she returned from the bathroom, and with it mopped up the various small swamps made by the spilled water. The polish on the bedside table had dulled from such constant accidents. While she drank her tea she settled down to read her library book, which was about Oliver Cromwell, a man she disliked. After a time she fell asleep, her glasses still on her nose and the bedside lamp burning, alone in the large house in its three acres of garden where she had lived for more than fifty years.

The next day was Thursday, one of Mrs Anderson's regular days for shopping in Framingham. Breakfast over, she put on her camel coat and a brown felt hat which she skewered to her thin hair with a long pin. She wrapped a scarf round her neck, zipped up her sheepskin boots and pulled on woollen gloves. Then she set off along the drive, through the gates which were left open for the milkman and the mail, and down Hatch Hill, trundling her wheeled shopping basket before her. Few cars passed her, for since the by-pass was built traffic on this road had dwindled.

At the foot of the hill, Mrs Anderson crossed the road and walked along the footpath until she reached the subway under the by-pass. Its cement walls were marked here and there with *graffiti*, but not a lot, for the population of Framingham was not much given to vandalism or vulgarity. The subway floor was tiled, and became slippery in wet weather; Mrs Anderson was always glad to emerge into daylight at the end. She propelled her basket up the slope and along the road to the High Street, passing Blewett's Garage on the corner. For years she had driven into Framingham in a solid saloon car, changed every few years, bought from and serviced by first Geoff Blewett, and then his son Dave.

She had not missed the car too much at first when she gave it up. The walk to the shops was only a mile, and three times a day the bus went past The Gables; but the by-pass changed all that, cutting the house off from the town, and the buses no longer went that way. With the closure of the old road, the distance on foot was almost doubled unless you took the path across the fields and through the chuchyard. Allington, the nearest large town, was twelve miles from Framingham, and Mrs Anderson no longer went there; there was nothing to go for now, since the cinema seemed to deal only with sex and horror and most of the shops belonged to various chains.

As she passed the garage, a short youth with long, straight, mouse-coloured hair was putting petrol in a yellow Chevette. Mrs Anderson walked on towards the butcher's shop where she bought a chop, a small piece of brisket and half a pound of sausages. Then she turned into Fresh Foods which had once belonged to Mr Gibson; gone were the days when she telephoned her weekly order and it was delivered, and she still found the supermarket system trying. Mrs Anderson parked her wheeled basket by the door and took a wire trolley round the shelves; a basket soon grew heavy even with only a few items. She collected tea, various tins to maintain her stocks in case she could not get out to the shops, butter, a loaf. She chose the check-out manned by the plump, spotty girl who was always patient and helpful, and was just manoeuvring her wheeled basket away from the till to the door when a brisk, impatient woman pushed past her, nearly knocking her over and then letting the door swing back upon her.

Another woman came up behind Mrs Anderson, caught the door and held it open for her, smiling, while Mrs Anderson trundled through.

''Oh — thank you,'' said Mrs Anderson, pushing her basket on to the pavement.

The woman was plump, middle-aged, and wore a dark sheepskin coat. She had a rather florid face and smoothly waved greying hair.

''Can you manage?'' she inquired, and when Mrs Anderson nodded and thanked her again, gave her another smile and walked away, her own basket over her arm, her legs in patterned tights sturdy beneath a

4

checked tweed skirt. She disappeared through a doorway further along the High Street, and passing later, on her way to the library, Mrs Anderson saw it was the office of the Women's Royal Voluntary Service.

She had not finished Oliver Cromwell, but she had another book to return, and before she selected one from the shelves she sat down in a comfortable chair with a tweed-covered seat and pine arms; it was a low chair, and without the arms, rising from it would have been difficult. Mrs Anderson sat there for some time, turning the pages of *Country Life* and resting. An old man and another old woman sat there too, the woman reading the local paper and the man openly dozing. Mrs Anderson did not know them but she often saw them in the library, passing the time and resting, like herself.

Later, as she walked back into the High Street and towards the turning to the subway, it began to rain. Kevin Timms, on his way to buy sandwiches from Takeaway Snax for his lunch, saw her turn the corner towards the underpass. In his mind he followed her home, as he had done that first time, up Hatch Hill and into the big house with its unused rooms where the furniture was shrouded in dustsheets and which he visited, at night, several times a week.

By the time Mrs Anderson emerged from the subway it was raining hard. She put up the umbrella which she kept in her shopping basket and trudged along the path towards the foot of Hatch Hill. As she began the slow haul up to The Gables she concentrated on pulling her load behind her and keeping the worst of the rain off

5

with the umbrella; there was no room in her mind for other thoughts and she did not notice the car that came up to her, slowing as it drew level. A voice called her several times but Mrs Anderson trudged on, and to win her attention the driver had to get out and hurry after her.

"Would you like a lift? Do let me take you home," said Muriel Dean, putting a hand on the old woman's arm to halt her. Rain pattered down on her grey waves and her dark sheepskin coat as Mrs Anderson hesitated. "Come along," urged Muriel. "Let me take your shopping."

"I'm only going to the top of the hill," said Mrs Anderson.

"Well, that's quite far enough in this downpour," said Muriel. She took the basket and opened the passenger door of the Maxi while Mrs Anderson lowered her umbrella and clambered awkwardly in.

"How very kind of you to stop," said Mrs Anderson as Muriel got in beside her. She peered at her benefactress, who had got quite wet in those few moments. "I don't think we've met."

"We did this morning," said Muriel. "In the supermarket." By now they had reached the top of the hill and she slowed up as she saw a gateway on the left. "Is this where you live?"

"Yes," said Mrs Anderson.

Muriel hid her surprise. The house was, she knew, owned by an old woman who was allegedly somewhat of a recluse; she had not expected this small, bent old person, whom she had often seen in the town, to be its occupant. She turned in at the gate and drove up the rutted, long and twisting drive, looking curiously at the large house, built in red brick in Victorian gothic style, as she stopped by the front door. She insisted on taking Mrs Anderson's shopping into the house for her. The old lady led the way round to the back door and Muriel watched as she took the key from under a stone near a water-butt. A long passage led from the back door into the house, and various doors opened off it; one, on the left, was the kitchen. It was large and warm, with an Aga stove and a big, scrubbed deal-topped table. There was a dresser against one wall, and in a corner, a leather armchair, rather worn and sagging.

"Let me make you a cup of tea while you take off your wet things," said Muriel, going at once to the stove and lifting the kettle. It was full and she put it on.

"Please don't trouble," Mrs Anderson said, standing small and rather defensive in front of her samaritan. "I've taken up enough of your time."

"It's no trouble," said Muriel. "And I'm not in a hurry."

Mrs Anderson was tired and wanted to give way to her fatigue, but would not do so before a witness. The quickest way to regain her privacy would be, she saw, to submit, so she went from the room and along the hall to the cloakroom, where she hung up her coat and hat and took off her boots, putting on soft flat-heeled shoes. She put her umbrella up and left it to dry on the tile floor. While she was doing all this, Muriel had explored the larder on the pretext of searching for milk. The refrigerator was a very old one, all motor and with scant storage space, but the larder was cool, with a mesh window, and slate shelves on which were stacked tins of mince, stew, salmon, vegetables, and dried milk. There was enough food to last for several weeks. Muriel took a bottle of milk from the refrigerator and found tea in a tin on the kitchen dresser. There were cups and saucers in one of the cupboards, and the teapot was at the side of the stove where it would always be warm. When Mrs Anderson returned, the kettle was boiling.

''We'll go into the sitting-room,'' said Mrs Anderson, her tone brusque because she saw two cups and saucers on the tray.

''You lead the way and I'll carry the tray,'' said Muriel, blithely unaware that she had outstayed her welcome.

As she followed Mrs Anderson into the hall, Muriel saw at the far end of it the front door, with panels of coloured glass above and on either side. Other doors led off the hall, and there was a wide staircase which made two turns before reaching the first floor. The room Mrs Anderson took her into was small. There were two armchairs and a chesterfield, an oak gatelegged table, a desk, a mahogany bookcase, and a colour television. In the hearth stood a paraffin heater which the old lady lit with a match from a box on the mantelpiece. There were two bowls of hyacinth bulbs on the window sill, the shoots just turning green, and on every shelf or space were ranged framed photographs, at which Muriel glanced curiously as she set down the tray. She picked up the milk jug and poured from it.

''Sugar?'' she asked.

Mrs Anderson felt like a guest in her own house.

"No, thank you," she said coldly.

"You live here alone?" Muriel asked.

"Yes."

"It's a very big house. I wonder you haven't thought of selling it."

"My family grew up here. I'm keeping it for my son," said Mrs Anderson. She sipped her tea, was glad of its warmth, and added more kindly, "I've had offers for the house, but I won't sell."

"Your son?" Muriel prompted.

"He's in Australia," said Mrs Anderson.

Muriel looked round at the ranks of photographs that stood on the mantelpiece, the bookcase, the top of the desk. Male faces stared back at her, small boys in shorts, and young men in uniform.

"That's Billy," Mrs Anderson said. She indicated a photograph in a silver frame on the mantelpiece. It showed a young man with a smile, a lot of dark, curly hair, and a moustache. "It was taken a long time ago. He's been in Australia for twenty-six years."

"And the others?" Muriel asked, now not just curious but genuinely interested.

"My other two sons were killed in the war," said Mrs Anderson. "Harry and Jack." She pointed out their photographs, a dark young man in naval uniform and a fairer one with a pilot's wings on his chest.

Muriel asked no more questions. She'd learn the rest another day.

"Thank you for bringing me home and making the tea," said Mrs Anderson, summoning graciousness. "It was most kind.'' She stood up and moved to the door.

Muriel allowed herself to be dismissed.

''I'll pop in again when I'm passing,'' she said, and misinterpreting Mrs Anderson's instant protesting gesture, added, ''No, really, I'd like to.''

Putting her chop in the oven late; Mrs Anderson knew that she would see the woman, who had said that her name was Muriel Dean, again, and sighed. She had so little spare energy for such encounters. But she had been glad of the ride up the hill.

It was years since she'd been in a car.

Kevin Timms, out of work again and loitering about the streets of Framingham, had noticed Mrs Anderson among the passing populace. Lounging against a wall with his feet stuck out in front of him, he did not move when she approached, pushing her wheeled shopping basket in front of her. She had looked at him, eyes faded blue in a lined face that was pale under the brim of her felt hat, as if she expected him to move out of her way, and she waited until, unwillingly, he did so. Afterwards, angry, he had followed her along the road and into the subway under the by-pass. It would be easy in the subterranean gloom to snatch her purse. But as he padded up behind her on soft rubber soles, someone came the other way and he fell back, following her at a distance along the footpath beside the by-pass and then up Hatch Hill until she turned in at The Gables.

He'd returned when it was dark, slipping up the drive to peer in at the one lighted window on the ground floor. Through a gap in the curtains he'd made out a sitting-room — the edge of a chair, a rug on the floor. As he watched, a figure passed across the room: the old woman. There were no other movements, and after a while Kevin realized that she was alone in the house. He waited on, shivering with excitement, crouched among bushes that bordered the drive, until the light downstairs went off and, some minutes later, another came on upstairs. Then he prowled round the house, trying the doors, front and back, and one that led into a conservatory, but all were locked. The big sash windows, however, looked easy. Kevin drew out the knife he always carried and tried one of them at the front of the house. He eased the blade between the frames of the window and slid the catch aside without difficulty. In seconds he was inside the room. He fished in his pocket for a box of matches and by the light of one made out the dim shapes of furniture covered with dustsheets.

He moved across and opened the door to the hall. A second match showed him more doors. As the matches burnt down, he put them out and replaced them carefully in the box; it was quite full, and he had another besides; Kevin always carried the means to fire. He opened a door at the end of the hall and found it led to the sitting-room he had observed from outside; there was the patterned rug. He went inside.

The room was warm. Kevin saw a paraffin heater in the hearth and lit it, then sat in an armchair. For a moment he contemplated what would happen if he tipped the heater so that the fuel ran over the floor. It would flare up like a bonfire, the same as that other time. He played with the idea of starting a blaze, but then turned out the fire. That could wait. He went into the hall and continued to explore. In the kitchen he inspected the Aga cooker, lifting the heavy covers over the hot plates to see how it worked. He saw all the tins in the larder, and the small, old-fashioned refrigerator, and eventually he came to the cloakroom, which was large, with a row of hooks against one wall on which hung a camel coat, a navy raincoat, some hats, a tweed cap, and three shabby jackets. There were boots, suede zipped ones lined with sheepskin, several pairs of wellingtons in various sizes. Some of the things were men's but Kevin felt convinced that the old woman was alone in the house. The lavatory door opened off the cloakroom in a small room to itself. Kevin stared, amazed, at the solid mahogany seat. He lifted it and urinated luxuriously, making his steaming mark. But he didn't flush it; she might hear. He lowered the seat again. She'd not notice, by morning. Old people didn't; they were all half blind.

Kevin was enjoying himself now. He went upstairs and tried the first door he came to. His flickering match showed him a bedroom with twin beds covered in checked dustsheets, and some heavy furniture. He tried all the doors on the landing and found five bedrooms, all empty and dust-sheeted, and two bathrooms, a large one at the front of the house and a smaller one at the back. Both had baths that stood on legs on green linoleum.

There was one door left at the end of the passage, near the smaller bathroom. That must be where she slept. No light showed beneath it. Kevin opened it quietly; there was no sound of breathing but he knew someone was there. She'd have money in the room, jewels, perhaps. But he didn't strike a match, not this time. He'd be coming again? He closed the door.

A flight of stairs led from this landing to one above, and as he looked up a draught of cold air blew out Kevin's match. He'd leave that, till he'd got a torch.

CHAPTER
TWO

"I met the old woman who lives in that big house on Hatch Hill today," Muriel Dean told her husband that evening.

"Oh?" Howard Dean did not look up from the papers he had taken from his briefcase. He brought work home not only because he had a lot of it, but as a defence against Muriel's perpetual torrent of speech. He recognized her qualities — her concern, actively demonstrated, for others — even her frustrations, since in him she must often be disappointed, but he found the unending flow of words she poured upon him whenever they were together exhausting.

"She must be over eighty," Muriel went on. "She had two sons killed in the war. I don't know how long she's been alone up there. Ages."

"Oh," said Howard again, making a note on a page.

Muriel sat with a glass of sherry facing him across the fireplace. She supposed he was listening as he leafed through his papers. He was forty-eight, and going a little bald, wearing now a shabby cardigan instead of the jacket of his pin-striped suit. He was the senior partner in a firm of solicitors in the City, and twelve years ago the family had moved from Ealing to this solid, square house with its large garden, so that the two daughters could benefit from country life. Every morning Howard caught the ten to eight train from Framingham station, which was five minutes' walk from Beech House.

"I was going to Dartworth, to lunch with Heather," Muriel persisted. "And I saw old Mrs Anderson dragging her shopping-basket up the hill, so I gave her a lift. Poor old thing, she looked exhausted, and it was pouring with rain."

Parts of her tale filtered through to Howard. Without looking up, he reached out for his sherry and sipped it. Muriel was due that evening at a meeting dedicated to keeping industry out of Framingham; he'd only to wait, and she'd be gone.

"She's got a son in Australia. She's keeping the house for him," Muriel said. "I don't suppose he'll ever want a barn of a place like that. He's been gone for twenty-six years. I'm going to see what I can do about it."

This threat got through to Howard. Muriel was going to meddle. She often did.

"Why shouldn't she stay where she is as long as she can?" he asked. "You wouldn't like to be turned out of this house, would you? Just because you were old?"

"There's quite a difference, darling," said Muriel. "You could put Beech House into that place several times over."

"Well, I expect she likes it," said Howard. "She's quite fit, isn't she?"

"For her age, yes," Muriel conceded. "Some of that generation are pretty tough."

"If you take away her home, you could take away her

reason for living,'' said Howard.

''Nonsense,'' said Muriel. ''She'd get a fortune for it and be able to go somewhere really nice — a hotel, say, until she gets too frail, then a nursing home.''

''You've got it all worked out, haven't you?'' Howard said, looking at her at last.

''I thought about it as I drove back this afternoon,'' Muriel said. ''I don't know how much help she has in the house — maybe none. I'll find out. And Meals on Wheels would be a good idea, if she isn't having them.''

Howard gave up. If Mrs Anderson had managed to survive for eighty years, she might be a match for Muriel's benevolence, though he feared that no one could really escape if she concentrated her full organizing abilities upon them. She had organized Howard at first, spurring a shy man to success. Then she had organized their daughters, Angela and Felicity, docile girls overshadowed by their forceful mother; both had fled into marriage before they were twenty. With the girls gone, Muriel had plenty of time to spare for charity and welfare work. Most people admired her; indeed, Howard respected her energy. Perhaps Mrs Andersen, destined to receive her kindly concern, would welcome it; she might be lonely. But she might not want to sell her house.

Muriel went off to her meeting at last, leaving Howard to enjoy his solitary casserole. He heard the car roar off up the road; she was an efficient driver but hard on the car. When she had gone, he finished his meal quickly, cleared it away and put the dishes in the dishwasher. Then, in a shabby raincoat and with a tweed hat on his head, he wheeled a bicycle out of the garage, turned on its dynamo-operated lights, and pedalled swiftly through Framingham towards an estate of small modern houses on the far side of the railway.

Four days after their meeting, Muriel called on Mrs Anderson. It was Monday, three weeks before Christmas, a cold day, dry but with a sharp north-east wind blowing. Muriel had spent the day at the Women's Royal Voluntary Service office where she worked twice a week, and whilst there had discovered that Mrs Anderson did not receive Meals on Wheels.

The days were short now and it was dusk when she turned through the gates and drove up the drive to The Gables. On her earlier visit she had noticed beds of rose bushes close to the house; beyond, lawns sloped away to an orchard and a copse. The grass had been cut, and the roses bore no dead heads. Perhaps there was a gardener. Muriel walked up the stone steps leading to the front door and rang the bell. She could hear it jangling somewhere at the back of the house, and after some delay a light came on in the hall.

Mrs Anderson had just settled down with a cup of tea and Story Time on the radio when the doorbell interrupted her. Her day was punctuated by various programmes on radio and television — the morning story on radio, news and certain sporting events on television. She had bought a new colour television set three years ago when her black-and-white one had been pronounced beyond repair. It had tempted her into spending more time viewing, teaching her a lot about other countries, insects and animals.

"Ah — Mrs Anderson, I came to see how you're getting along," Muriel boomed heartily when she opened the door. Most old people were deaf, and in case this one was also forgetful, reminded her, "You remember — I brought you home the other day — Thursday, when it was so wet." As she spoke she surged over the threshold into the hall, took hold of the door which Mrs Anderson still held, and closed it, saying, "We don't want to let the cold in, do we? It's cold enough as it is."

And indeed it was bitter in the hall. Used to her centrally heated house, Muriel looked round and saw an old-fashioned radiator against one wall. She took off a sheepskin glove and touched it as she passed: icy.

Retreating before her, Mrs Anderson was forced to conduct Muriel to her sitting-room. She turned off the radio and said, "I was just going to have tea. One moment while I fetch another cup."

Muriel looked at the tray. There was a digestive biscuit on a plate beside teapot and milk jug.

"I'll get it — don't you stir," she said. "I know the way, and was off to the kitchen before her involuntary hostess could protest.

Muriel soon learned that Mrs Anderson did not wish to receive Meals on Wheels.

"It's not charity," Muriel assured her. "You pay. But it's not expensive and it saves you cooking." Old people had their pride. "Shopping must be a problem for you."

"I manage well," Mrs Anderson told her. "I've

nothing else to do now but look after myself.'' Till Billy comes back, she added to herself.

''I think you're wonderful,'' Muriel said, and meant it. ''How do you manage the garden? It looks trim near the house.''

''I keep those beds myself,'' said Mrs Anderson. ''And grow a few vegetables. Not as many as I did. Mr Knox, who delivers the paraffin, cuts the grass for me.''

Joe Knox had offered to do it, some years ago, seeing her struggling. He brought his own powerful machine.

''What about help in the house?'' Muriel pursued, and was told that Mrs Clarke came once a week, on Fridays.

''It's quite enough,'' said Mrs Anderson. ''I use only a few rooms.''

''Whereabouts in Australia is your son?'' asked Muriel, and was told he travelled a lot. Mrs Anderson had never been out to see him; she'd expected to at first, but thought it best to wait until he settled. Now she was too old.

''But you aren't,'' said Muriel. ''You'd be looked after very well on the trip, flying. It would be easier than going to Framingham to shop.''

''I'm too old for a first flight,'' said Mrs Anderson firmly.

She would not reveal to anyone that Billy had never suggested she should go, not even long ago, in the first years.

Muriel left at last, promising to return, and Mrs Anderson recognized that when she said a thing, she meant it.

*   *   *

Howard Dean first met Janet Finch when an accident blocked the railway line near Framingham and buses took passengers round the obstruction. He sat next to her in the bus, calm himself at the delay, and found that she was not. Fretting, consulting her watch, she sat tense in her seat as though to push the bus onwards by her own willpower. Howard at last spoke.

"We'll only be about twenty minutes late," he said. "The train's not always punctual."

She gave a sudden breathless laugh and slumped back against the upholstery.

"I know — it's always a worry — I'm usually on an earlier train," she said, and then, turning to look at him, added, "It's my daughter — I'm never at home when she gets back from school as it is."

"How old is she?" asked Howard. The girl herself looked little older than his own daughters, clasping her large handbag now with a nervous tautness.

"She's nine," said Janet.

"You work in town?"

She did not travel to the end of the line, only as far as a suburb where she was personal assistant to the managing director of a plastics firm. Her brother-in-law had helped her to find the job when her marriage broke up; she'd lived in Framingham for some years before that, and now she had a mortgage on a small house in Fowler's Piece, near the station.

At first, Howard thought his interest was simply because Janet reminded him of his own daughters. After they parted, he thought about her and wished he knew her name. Since she normally travelled up by a later train than his, and returned earlier, they were not likely to meet again. Then, two weeks after their meeting, he caught an earlier train himself because he had a bad cold and, after sneezing in the office all day, decided to take his germs and his shivers home. She was walking down the platform at Framingham ahead of him, a thin, dark girl with curly hair, long legs in neat boots. He hurried to catch up with her.

''How's your daughter?'' he asked.

Janet paused by the steps to the footbridge over the line. She recognized him at once and smiled. He thought her very pretty, something he did not remember noticing before.

''Oh, fine,'' she replied.

''I've been thinking about you,'' said Howard. ''Are you sure you've received proper advice?''

She looked surprised.

''My brother-in-law has done all he could,'' she said.

''I didn't mean that,'' said Howard. ''I'm sure he has. I just wondered if there wasn't some way you could spend more time at home. Look, here's my card. I'm a solicitor.'' He fished in his wallet. ''Ring me at my office if you think I could help.'' He sneezed then, shatteringly, said goodbye and walked off, leaving her staring after him.

She telephoned the next week.

CHAPTER
THREE

Kevin returned to the big house on Hatch Hill the night after his first visit. This time he brought a torch. He waited in the garden until no lights showed, then climbed in as he had done before. He looked round the rooms he had already seen, and when he came to Mrs Anderson's door he paused, listening. There was no sound. He turned the handle cautiously and gently pushed the door open. With his fingers over the bulb, filtering the light, Kevin shone his torch round the room and on to the high bed. The old woman lay there, one fist at her cheek, her thin white hair straggling over the pillow, and at first he thought she was not breathing; he moved towards her, looking down at her, and saw her shoulder lift slightly. He thought he had never seen anyone so old; she looked like a sort of rag doll.

Her handbag was on a chest of drawers and he opened it. There was a purse inside, with some coins in it and three pounds in single notes. He took two of them and then tiptoed out of the room and closed the door. Then he went up the second flight of stairs to the top landing, where he found three small rooms. In one, there was a cupboard full of toys — clockwork and electric trains of what looked to Kevin antique make, a fort and

22

toy soldiers, model cars and boxes of games. There was a dappled rocking-horse with threadbare grey mane and tail in a corner. The other rooms each held a narrow iron bedstead with a horsehair mattress, a white-painted washstand with a china bowl and a jug on it and drawers beneath, and a small wardrobe. The floorboards were stained dark brown and there was one small mat by the bed in each room.

Kevin flung himself down on one of the beds, arms up under his head, his thin body stretched out, knowing power. He could smother the old woman lying downstairs and she would never know who had attacked her. He could take over the house and make it his kingdom.

Kevin lived with his aunt Jessie Swales, who had given him a home since his mother died in a fire when he was twelve. Kevin often dreamed about that night, the flames leaping and licking around the small terraced house, the clanging bells of the fire brigade, and the man, Len, his hair and eyebrows singed, face blackened, weeping. Kevin's father had left home long before, and no one would tell Kevin where he had gone. It was boys at school who had said that he was in prison.

Jessie was his mother's younger sister. She lived in Allington, in what had been the family home, a small house among rows of semi-detached pairs in an old part of the town. Jessie worked for the electricity board, where she had begun as an insignificant office girl, learning typing at night school. She paid a neighbour to take Kevin in after school and in the holidays, until her return from work, and in the evenings she helped him with his homework and tried to waken ambition in him, but Kevin had little interest in work of any sort, either at school or later. Small and weedy, he was picked on by other boys and bullied. He learned to fight back, but fought foul and exacted revenge by devious means, scribbling in his enemies' exercise books, damaging their bikes, setting fire to the waste-paper basket in the classroom when he was kept in. He was always in trouble.

Jessie tried to be patient and blamed his shortcomings on the circumstances; his lapses were her failures. She was relieved when he left school without getting caught for some serious offence; there had been acts of vandalism near the school, walls daubed with painted slogans, windows broken with stones, lighted paper pushed through letter-boxes, and she feared, dreaded, that Kevin might have been involved. She got him his first job, in a hardware store in Allington. Kevin lasted there for just six weeks, tolerated only so long because the shopkeeper respected his aunt and hoped that his unpunctuality and surliness would improve. They never did, and when money began to disappear from the till, Kevin was dismissed.

After that he drifted from job to job and was out of work more often than not, until at last he was taken on at a factory two miles outside Framingham, travelling each way on a works bus. Then, one Saturday, hanging about in the car park behind a big supermarket in Allington, he saw a woman leave her car unlocked while she pushed her wire trolley back to the doorway of the shop. In seconds Kevin was reaching into the car. Her open handbag lay on the seat, just asking to be ransacked. He snatched her purse and was gone, out of the park and round the corner, before she came back to the car. The purse held fifty pounds in ten and five pound notes. Kevin took the money and tossed the purse over a wall into a nearby builder's yard.

He used the money for a down payment on an old, not very powerful motor-bike and travelled to work independently from then onwards. He was quite good with his hands and soon understood how the bike worked and how to fit various spare parts when required. Jessie was thankful when he found this new interest; he tinkered with the bike at weekends and went off for rides; she postponed, yet again, asking him to help with the household expenses although he was holding down his job, hoping that her worries were over.

It was surprising how easily you could pick up a pound or two, and other things. Kevin never missed a chance, once he had started stealing from the till in his first job. At the factory, his workmates' coats, hanging on hooks, often held money, loose coins in pockets or an occasional note. At weekends he hung about in car parks looking for unlocked cars and often finding them. He won a good leather jacket like that, and a transistor radio, and once a pretty silk scarf which he'd taken home and given to his aunt. She'd been most touched, thinking he'd bought it specially.

Kevin never stole from Jessie, though it would have been easy, not even when she began to go out with Mr Watson.

He couldn't believe it, when he found out. Old Watson

called for her one Sunday in his white Cortina and took her off to the coast. She'd left Kevin a shepherd's pie in the oven and a piece of fruit tart. He never before remembered her leaving him on a Sunday; there had always been a roast for the two of them, sometimes with her friend Evie Kent from the office joining them. Kevin felt first abandoned, then furiously angry. When Jessie came home flushed and happy, and invited Bob Watson in for coffee, Kevin had refused to speak to either of them and had flung out of the house, roaring off up the road on his bike and not returning until long after Bob had gone.

Jessie was forty-two, a small, slight woman with faded brown hair and an anxious expression. Her youth had been spent looking after first an invalid father and then her nephew, working conscientiously meanwhile and rising slowly upwards in rank at the electricity board, where Bob was in the finance department. Their acquaintance was slight and casual for years; then Bob's wife died, and he, nearing retirement and lonely, began to look with more attention at the quiet, neat little woman who had been part of the background to his work for so long, and at last to ask her out.

Jessie rebuked Kevin for his rudeness.

"I was ashamed of you," she said.

"He's a silly, fat bugger," said Kevin. "What d'you want to go wasting your time with an old man like that for?"

"He's not an old man." Jessie rounded on him. "I've given you a good home all these years. I'm entitled to friends of my own, someone to think of me for a change.'' She'd rushed from the room before Kevin should see her tears, and he'd been left feeling frightened. What if she married the old geyser? Then where would he, Kevin, be?

A few days later, Kevin was made redundant at work. The factory had lost a big contract and had to reduce its work force. The last to be taken on were the first out. Kevin's compensation pay kept him going and he did not tell Jessie what had happened. His money was running out and it looked as if, in spite of social security, he would not be able to keep up the payments on his bike when he first noticed Mrs Anderson, followed her home, and broke into her house.

On his second visit, feeling hungry as he lay on the bed in the attic room, he remembered the stores in her larder. He went downstairs, put on the light in the kitchen, and helped himself to a tin of beans, which he heated on the stove, and a banana. He found an opener and cutlery in a drawer. He washed up carefully, and threw the tin into the dustbin outside the back door, bolting the door again after him as the old woman had done before going to bed.

Kevin went to the house every night that week, and by the end of it he'd made one of the attic bedrooms very comfortable. He'd taken up an electric fire from one of the first-floor bedrooms and plugged it in. He took up a lamp, too, and laid a magazine over the shade to mask the light, for the curtains were only flimsy cotton; but there was anyway small chance of it being seen outside, for the house was barely visible from the road. He took his transistor radio with him when he went to The

Gables, and lay on the bed while Mrs Anderson slept below, reading the girlie magazines he dare not let Jessie see and listening to pop music.

At the end of the first week, after a row of ruined suppers dried up in the oven, Jessie told him she would no longer provide an evening meal; if he wanted one, he must prepare it himself.

"I'm glad you've been meeting friends," she said, assuming this was the reason for his absence.

He let it go. There was always plenty of food in Jessie's store cupboard; he wouldn't need to go shopping.

So began his visits to The Gables, and in the second week he got a job at Blewett's Garage. He'd seen it advertised in the local paper. Dave Blewett knew about the redundancies; it was hard for a young lad when a thing like that happened, and he took Kevin on, despite some misgivings for the boy seemed surly. He displayed a certain grasp of simple mechanics and Dave hoped that, given a chance, he would shape up and perhaps be some use in the workshop.

Blewett's Garage stayed open for petrol until eight; they opened early, too, and were much used by commuters. Kevin and another lad worked alternate shifts, week about, late and early. When business was slack, Kevin lounged in the office reading a comic; the other boy did odd jobs in the workshop. When Kevin came off the early shift, he bought fish and chips and ate them in the bushes at The Gables, waiting till he could go into the house. On late nights he hadn't long to wait for the old woman to go to bed. Then he'd enter, go upstairs to his attic lair and lie on the bed reading his magazines, listening to pop, until long after midnight.

Kevin met Marilyn Green in a Framingham coffee bar. Most days, for lunch, he bought sandwiches at Takeaway Snax and ate them in the office, but sometimes he went to the coffee bar opposite Framingham station. He would sit at a corner table, head down, discouraging talk from other customers, and he'd ignore anyone else at his table. Once, when leaving, he accidentally knocked into another youth, making him spill his coffee.

"Do you mind?" said the youth, who was taller than Kevin, dressed in a donkey jacket, broad-shouldered and tough, a building labourer on a short job in the town. He put down his cup and squared up aggressively. Kevin slunk off, muttering. At the doorway a girl, also leaving, said consolingly, "I saw that. It wasn't your fault." A blush flooded her pallid face.

Kevin made no response, not even looking at her.

"That fellow. It was his fault," Marilyn Green persevered.

"Oh — him. Yeah," said Kevin, and slouched off up the road.

Marilyn watched him go, sighing, and walked slowly back to Fresh Foods, where she worked at the check-out.

CHAPTER
FOUR

When Janet telephoned him at the office, Howard Dean wasted no time. He went to see her the same evening, going straight to her house from the station. She had had to take time off from work because Laura, her daughter, had measles, and her employer, though sympathetic, was fretting because he had had to engage a temporary assistant who did not understand the work.

"I'll have to give it up, but how shall we manage?" Janet said. "I don't see how you can help — I shouldn't have called you. But it was your idea."

"I meant it," said Howard earnestly. He smiled at her, serious and kind. "You'll have to tell me about your assets."

Janet produced papers and revealed facts. Her ex-husband paid a small amount of maintenance for Laura but was often late and Janet was sure that eventually this support would dwindle away; she gave no explanation of their differences, concentrating on practicalities. From the sale of their joint home, she had received enough for a deposit on this house, and had been granted a mortgage on the strength of her job. Howard worked out the cost of her fares, and of paying someone to look after Laura in the school holidays as she had to sometimes, although often friends helped. He demonstrated that she could be just as well off with a job that paid less if she did not have to travel; peace of mind was worth pounds, Howard told her gravely, though it didn't pay the mortgage.

A few days later he introduced her to Emily Tarratt, a widow whom he and Muriel had known for years. Emily wanted to open a gift shop in Framingham and needed a partner. Framingham was a prosperous little town whose population was mainly middle-class, commuting to London or employed locally. There was scope for a shop of good taste selling craft work, china and glass. Howard could not imagine Emily associated with any sort of failure; she had carried out market research and was held back only by the lack of suitable premises, and someone to help with a pleasant disposition, but not necessarily any capital.

Emily took to Janet straight away. They were of different generations, but alike in many ways, practical and shrewd. Janet showed Emily patchwork cushions and a quilt that she had made, and a bear she had bought years before for Laura from a woman in Framingham who liked making soft toys. The lease of a shop in a good position near the centre of the High Street was about to expire and it would be available; Howard, who knew the estate agent dealing with it, secured it for them on better terms than Emily had anticipated, a local carpenter made the fitments, and they decorated it themselves. After rejecting various whimsical names for the shop, they called it Pandora, for within you might find anything, and opened, without fuss, one April day in time for Easter.

Now Laura came from school straight to the shop, had tea and did her homework in a room behind where there was a sink and a desk for business, and a small electric stove. There was a yard at the back where she could play and her friends loved coming there. Sometimes, and particularly on Saturdays, she went to a friend's house, and once, when she was ill, Emily managed without Janet. Another time, when Emily had bronchitis, Janet carried on alone. In theory, each had a day off every week, though in practice both were so attached to the business that they did not always take it, but the arrangement worked well.

In the first year, they had broken even and now were showing a good profit. Framingham's residents wondered how they had ever managed before Pandora opened. Janet had found local workers to supply them with craft goods: carved animals made by a retired schoolmaster; handwoven scarves and stoles; soft toys and pottery. She had lost her worried frown and put on weight; Laura was doing well at school; and Emily's tireless energy was now absorbed.

"I can never thank you enough for putting me in touch with Emily," Janet told Howard one summer evening. He had developed a habit of calling in, on Friday evenings, at the small house in Fowler's Row to see how things were going. At first he stayed only a short time, accepting a glass of sherry while he heard about the week's events. But this Friday he brought a bottle of sherry for Janet, as he sometimes did, and disclosed that Muriel was away visiting one of their daughters. Janet at once invited him to stay to supper, and he agreed without hesitation. He played Snap with Laura while Janet prepared the meal, and when Laura was in bed, he and Janet sat talking in the living-room with the windows open to the summer night. The scent of honeysuckle drifted in, and as the light faded, Janet grew confidential. She told him about the disillusion of her marriage: when he had married her, Desmond lost his interest in her; it was the chase that intrigued him, and when she was duly snared he seemed to think she needed nothing from him. All he appeared to want was a decorative and competent home manager while he hunted elsewhere. At last it became too much, a wearing-down, a loss of self.

It was quite dark by the time Howard got up to go.

"I've bored you," Janet said. "Sitting here without putting on the light, pouring out my troubles."

"You haven't. I'm just so sorry," Howard said. He heard similar tales, and many much worse, in his office all the time. He moved towards her in the gloom. "Things are better now," he stated. "You must put it all behind you, though I know it isn't easy." Her face was a pale blob as be addressed her earnestly. "I'm always here," he said, and without, as it seemed to him, planning it all, he kissed her, aiming in paternal fashion at her cheek.

But Janet turned her mouth to him.

He left two hours later, in a state of astounded, slightly shocked delight, walking home through the silent streets telling himself that it had happened only because Janet was grateful to him, and lonely, and that it would never be repeated.

But it was. Often.

Muriel never wasted time. The day after her visit to Mrs Anderson, she went to see Bryan Walsh, Framingham's main estate agent. At one time she had hoped her younger daughter, Felicity, would marry the Walshes' son, but instead she had married a Scottish engineer she met on holiday and now lived in Edinburgh.

Bryan sighed when his secretary told him who wanted him. Muriel would have come to browbeat him into performing some unwelcome good deed, he felt sure; he had already consented to be Father Christmas at a party she was organizing for a children's home. It was no good inventing an appointment; she was too persistent and would make one of her own. Perhaps she only wanted a cheque. He instructed that she should be admitted.

"It's about The Gables, Bryan," said Muriel, when his secretary had closed the door upon them. "You know it, don't you? That vast Victorian pile on Hatch Hill."

"Oh, I know The Gables," said Bryan. "Mrs Anderson."

"That's it."

"What about it?"

"What would it be worth?"

"Oh — " Bryan waved his hands vaguely. "A lot," he said. What was she thinking of? Surely she didn't plan to move Howard out of Beech House and off to the top of Hatch Hill?

"It's much too big for one old lady," said Muriel. "She ought to sell it and move into something smaller, or a home."

"I've asked her if she'd like to part with it more than once," said Bryan. "But she won't. She has a sentimental attachment to it. Lived there for most of her married life, hasn't she?"

Muriel had no time for sentiment.

"I'm sure I'll be able to persuade her to change her mind," she said. "I'd just like some idea of the price she'd get."

"Difficult to say," said Bryan. "A consortium wanted it for a country club just after old Mr Anderson died but she wouldn't hear of it. That was ages ago — before you came to Framingham, I think. It's not everybody's fancy, stuck on its own up there, and I bet it wants a lot done to it. The best bet would probably be a property developer who'd pull the house down and build an estate."

"Homes for young people," said Muriel. "I hadn't thought of that. It's an argument that might appeal to the old soul."

If anyone could persuade Mrs Anderson to sell, it would be Muriel, Bryan thought. She never gave up. He brightened at the prospect of a lucrative deal.

"Would a developer get the necessary planning consent?" Muriel asked.

"I should think so, because it's already residential," said Bryan.

"A hundred thousand pounds?" said Muriel.

"That's just for starters," said Bryan.

"I'll be in touch," Muriel promised, rising.

Bryan got up too, to show her out. He wouldn't take bets on the outcome of a battle between doughty old Mrs Anderson and tenacious Muriel, but it would certainly be a struggle of giants.

Mrs Anderson sat at her desk writing to Billy. Every week she covered two airmail pages with cheerful invented news. This week, she had a truthful story to relate: her encounter with Muriel Dean and the lift home she had been given.

I'd missed the bus, she wrote, to explain why she was walking. Billy need not know about the new, inconvenient route the bus took. *Mrs Dean is married to a solicitor who goes to London every day. They have two married daughters.* Muriel had interspersed her questions to Mrs Anderson with items of information about herself. The Deans had no grandchildren yet, and nor had she. She wouldn't mention that to Billy; it was too painful. His marriage had ended in divorce, poor boy, long ago, before he emigrated. She did not know what had become of his pretty, pale wife. She tried to imagine him as he would look now. Would he be bald, or have grey hair? A fat paunch or a lean frame? She sighed, unable to picture him, and looked instead at a photograph on her desk from which he gazed at her with a trustful, steady expression.

With an effort, Mrs Anderson bent to her letter again. She mentioned the weather — grey and cold, but that was to be expected so near Christmas. What would Billy be doing for Christmas, she asked him in the letter, and said that she would enclose her annual cheque in it, since parcels were not easy. Strange to think that his Christmas would be spent in hot weather, she remarked, as she did every year. In such a climate he wouldn't want handknitted sweaters or socks. During the last war, a tireless flow of such garments, seaboot stockings in oiled wool, and balaclava helmets, had poured from Mrs Anderson's busy needles, constructed in her spare time. The Gables had been a hostel for nurses working at Framingham Hospital. A housing estate now occupied the site of the hospital and its grounds, and under the centralization of public services the sick populace went to the new Allington General Hospital.

In 1941 Mrs Anderson's second son, Jack, who was in the navy, had married one of the nurses; they were both killed in a bombing raid on London, on a weekend's leave. Mrs Anderson had worked at the hospital, in what was then the almoner's department. Her husband, too old for the services, had been a part-time air raid warden. His business, a family one making furniture, had been switched to munitions. After the war, the change back to furniture had been difficult and slow, but there were profits from the war years to be put into development; the firm expanded and went public, and Mrs Anderson's main income still came from the shares.

She remembered all this, sitting at her desk, thinking of her dead sons. They seemed much closer now even than her husband. He had died of cancer in the big front bedroom at The Gables, nursed by her through terrible months of suffering. Afterwards she gradually moved out of the main rooms of the house, year by year using less of it until she achieved her present encampment in the kitchen, the small sitting-room and her room upstairs. Once, long ago, there were maids who slept on the top floor and a daily woman for the rough; now there was just Mrs Clarke, lethargically, on Fridays.

Mrs Anderson picked up her pen.

Once Christmas is over, the days grow longer and soon there will be snowdrops, she wrote. *I often think of the happy times when you were all young with your Christmas stockings to open.* Then, lest that sound melancholy, she added, *I am out a great deal, seeing friends, and may go away for Christmas.* Useless to write, *I wish you could be here.*

I am warm, she continued. *Paraffin for the stove is delivered once a week and as you know the Aga runs on oil. I have enough to last the winter. Sometimes there are strikes and shortages.* She went on to tell him that the Christmas rose near the front door had several buds, and ended, *Your loving Mother.*

She read the letter through, addressed the long blue envelope and put her own name and address in block capitals on the back. There were some stamps in a drawer of her desk and she stuck one ‹on, a special Christmas issue with an elaborate design. Then she put the letter on the table ready to post the next day when she went shopping. There was no pillar box within a mile.

For lunch she made an omelette; then she sat down to do the crossword in the *Daily Telegraph*. A boy on his way to school delivered the papers and in bad weather did not go to The Gables. In the school holidays, too, he rarely came. Mrs Anderson paid the newsagent in Framingham at the end of each month, and had given up complaining. The proprietor said it was difficult to get boys to go all the way up Hatch Hill just for her. She kept a record of what was delivered so that she was not overcharged. On Sundays no papers came at all. Mrs Anderson began to nod over the crossword, and soon she dozed. At half-past two the laundry man called, the same cheerful roundsman who had come for the past ten years, a young man when he began and now married, with three children. Mrs Anderson sent most of her washing to the laundry, though it was expensive and they often lost or tore things. Mrs Clarke had suggested dripdry sheets and a washing machine, but Mrs Anderson said the cost of the machine and the sheets would pay for a lot of laundry, and at her time of life she did not intend to learn to work a machine. Mrs Clarke, who patronized the launderette herself, offered to do the washing in the course of her duties, planning to bring her own with her to do in her employer's time and at her expense, but Mrs Anderson preferred things as they were.

Mrs Anderson had just settled down to play patience until it was time for the radio play when the front door bell rang. Muriel Dean stood on the step, paper bag in hand.

"I was just passing," she announced, stepping firmly in. "I brought you a little present — a cake from Wendy's. They're so delicious."

Wendy's was an expensive café and *pâtisserie* much frequented for morning coffee by Framingham matrons.

The gift disarmed Mrs Anderson. As on the earlier occasion, she retreated through the hall while Muriel advanced, parcel to the fore.

"I'll just slip off my coat," she said, laying her sheepskin on a chair in the hall. "I hope my boots won't mark the floor."

"Never mind," said Mrs Anderson, leading the way into the sitting-room. As before, she switched off the radio.

Muriel noticed the airmail envelope on the table as she sat down near the heater.

"This is a good fire," she said. "And economical, I expect."

"Yes," agreed Mrs Anderson.

"Your cleaning woman — will she come extra if you're not well?" Muriel inquired.

"I doubt it — I haven't asked," said Mrs Anderson. Occasionally she got a cold, which she dosed with aspirin and whisky; her stiff joints were the penalty of age. "My health is good," she added.

"Who's your doctor?"

"Some new young man — Bate — Barnes — I've never met him," said Mrs Anderson. "Dr Fosdyke retired."

"Dr Baynes, you mean," said Muriel. "We go to him. He's excellent."

"I don't like changes," said Mrs Anderson, who did not like all these questions, either. Yet, in a way, it was pleasant to be paid attention, to have a friendly face intently turned to one; and Mrs Dean meant to be kind.

"I was talking to a friend the other day," Muriel said.

40

"Bryan Walsh — perhaps you know him, he's an estate agent. He said he had several clients who are looking out for places like this one and willing to pay a lot for them. A hundred thousand pounds at least, as a speculation."

"You mean to pull the house down and put up a lot of jerry-built chicken coops instead."

"Well — they'd be homes for young people," Muriel pointed out. "And you'd be able to go to a — a hotel. Somewhere where you'd be looked after."

For a moment a vision came to Mrs Anderson: a smiling girl bringing her breakfast on a tray, perhaps someone else as old as herself to talk to. She banished it.

"What would I do all day?" she asked. "I'd get lazy. I should wither away."

"I don't think you would," said Muriel. "Things would be easier for you, that's all."

"I know the house is worth a lot," Mrs Anderson said. "And the longer I keep it, the more its value will increase. Billy will have something worth inheriting when I die."

With rare restraint, Muriel decided that she had said enough for now; she'd return to the attack another time.

"Let me get some tea," she suggested. "You sit still and rest." She went out of the room, carrying the paper bag containing the cake.

While she was gone, Mrs Anderson switched on the radio play, the volume low. It had promised to be a good one, about India under the Raj; she'd been looking forward to it. But Muriel was not long; she soon returned with a tray and the cake was certainly delicious, iced coffee sponge.

"Wendy's cakes are beautifully fresh. It will keep for days," said Muriel, cutting each of them a slice.

"It's kind of you to think of it," said Mrs Anderson. "Thank you." To make conversation, she asked where Muriel lived; she knew Grove Road, near the station in a quiet area.

"There's been a lot of building in the town," said Muriel. "That estate the other side of the railway, Fowler's Piece, for example — small houses, hugger mugger."

"Yet you want me to sell this, so that other small houses can be built here," Mrs Anderson challenged her.

"This is a long way from the town. There's space here to expand," said Muriel promptly. "Why don't you ask your son about it? See what he thinks?"

"I've always made my own mind up," said Mrs Anderson severely.

Muriel took the tray out and washed up what they had used. She put the cake in a tin in the larder. Mrs Anderson left her to it, switching on the play again; protest was useless in the face of such determination. When Muriel returned to the sitting-room, she affected to notice the airmail letter on the table for the first time.

"Shall I post it for you?" she offered. "If I put it in the box at the post office as I go by, it will go tonight. I have to pass it on my way home."

It would be insulting to refuse. Mrs Anderson thanked her for her thoughtfulness.

Before she dropped the letter into the box at the post office, Muriel carefully copied Billy's address into her engagement diary.

CHAPTER
FIVE

After their meeting at the coffee bar, Marilyn Green spent a lot of time thinking about the boy she had spoken to by the door. She read love stories in magazines and longed for a prince charming to carry her off to a castle of dreams. He did not have to be tall and handsome, for she was far from beautiful. The next time he went to the coffee bar she saw him as soon as she entered, and greatly daring, sat at his table. Shy girls should remember that boys can be just as shy, her weekly magazine had told her. Kevin did not glance at her, intent on his beans on toast, but she did not mind; she'd break the ice.

"Nice day, isn't it?" she said, and sank her teeth into a soft roll filled with egg and tomato. A wisp of cress caught at the side of her mouth and she fished for it with her large, spatulate tongue.

Kevin did not answer. He stared at the strong coffee in the cup before him, and Marilyn chewed on through several more mouthfuls.

"What're you doing for Christmas?" she asked, a little desperately.

Kevin looked at her at last. He saw the plain, fat face, the brown eyes, small anxious buttons set in folds of flesh, a pimple on her chin. Kevin had never had a girl friend; he'd been to discos but had not found a girl to leave with him. Now he had the wit to realize that this pasty girl had few chances either. Well, she wasn't anything to shout about, it was true, but she'd probably got most of the right things in the right places, and she'd be a pushover, for sure.

"Don't know," he said.

Marilyn waited for him to ask her plans, and when he didn't, she told him.

"I won't be doing anything special. Just staying with me mum and dad." And they'd be out most of the time, if past years were anything to go by. Her mother worked in the kitchen at the Rose and Crown, and her father was fond of the bar. "I live in Hawk's Row," Marilyn went on. "D'you know where that is? Past the railway, beyond Fowler's Piece. A row of old houses, it is, but quite nice. I've always lived there."

She stopped talking to finish her roll, and Kevin stood up.

"I've got to go," he said.

"Oh — see you, then," said Marilyn.

"Yeah." If he wanted to, he'd find her here, easy enough; that was certain.

It was over a week before they met again. This time Kevin looked up when she came to his table; he watched while she took off her green and orange checked coat which was made of some sort of blanket-like fabric and had a hood. As she sat down, her fat body quivered.

"Well," she said, panting slightly. She'd hurried, full of hope that he might be there, as she did every day.

Kevin ate another mouthful of sausage and mash. The coffee bar menu was limited; sometimes there was shepherd's pie or spaghetti bolognese, but the main fare was rolls and sandwiches. Today, Marilyn had a cheese roll. Kevin watched her large mouth open, the insertion of the roll, and the great bite. The muscles in her jaw worked hard as she chewed.

"Where d'you work, then?" he asked.

"Fresh Foods," said Marilyn. "I'm on the check-out, mostly."

"Oh."

"Where do you?"

"What?"

"Work."

"In the motor trade," said Kevin grandly.

"Oh — you're an engineer then," said Marilyn, impressed.

"Sort of," said Kevin. "I've got a bike."

He spoke nicely, she noticed.

"Lovely." Marilyn imagined herself riding pillion, hair streaming in the wind as she clutched the waist of her gallant knight.

Her gallant knight said, unenthusiastically, "Like to go to the pictures? There's *Horror at Midnight* on in Allington."

"When do you mean?" Excitement made her heart beat faster.

"Saturday," said Kevin.

"I don't mind." She mustn't seem too eager.

"Pick you up at half seven," Kevin said. "At the station."

He got up, and without another word to her, left the coffee bar. Marilyn finished the éclair which rounded off her meal in an agitated manner. Did he mean it? Why couldn't he pick her up at home? He knew where she lived. She didn't even know his name.

On Saturday evening, Kevin went home at the end of the early shift in two minds about going back to fetch the girl. He'd enjoy the film just as much on his own. Jessie was in the kitchen, whisking up cream in a bowl, when he got in. A bottle of Spanish red wine was open on the kitchen table and lightly fried chicken joints, surrounded by button mushrooms and small carrots, lay in an open casserole.

"Smells good." Kevin picked up the bottle of wine, put it to his lips, and slurped some down.

"Kevin, don't do that! Put it down." Jessie snatched the bottle from him. "And don't put your hands in there." Kevin was sticking a dirty finger into a bowl containing a dark, chocolate mixture. "I'm having a friend in," she said. "Aren't you going out? You always do, on Saturday." She'd banked on it, when inviting Bob.

"Cool it. I'm going to the pictures with a bird," said Kevin airily. "You're not the only one, you know, you and your fucking mister God almighty."

"Kevin, don't use that language to me," said Jessie, but Kevin was not staying to listen. He stuck his finger in the bowl of whipped cream and scooped some of it out, licking it as he slouched from room and thumped noisily upstairs. Soon Jessie heard the bathwater running. Kevin liked washing; he had a bath whenever he got home, however late it was, even in the middle of the night. Jessie sighed. The water wouldn't have heated up again in time for her, before Bob came.

Kevin, in a clean shirt and jeans beneath his jacket, set off slowly for his appointment. It would do the stupid bitch good to wait. He stopped in a quiet spot to take off his L plates, for that was asking for trouble — taking a bird on a bike with them on. Then, afraid that after all she might not be there, he accelerated for the last part of the journey, arriving at the station with a roar.

She was waiting beside a poster advertising bargain railway holidays, wearing her thick, blanket-like coat with its vivid pattern. Kevin had "borrowed" a helmet for her from Blewett's, for the law would be looking out for any sort of chance to get at someone who was just minding his own business. He'd taken five quid out of the till, too. He unbuckled the helmet from behind the seat and gave it to her. It was orange, like her coat.

Marilyn put it on, fumbling with the strap and seeming, to Kevin, to take for ever. Then she gingerly approached the bike, put her hand on his arm and her stout leg in its zipped boot across the pillion. He showed her where to put her feet.

"There's no need to hold on to me," he said, feeling her arms round his waist. But Marilyn was too nervous to let go. She clung to him as they sped through the outskirts of Framingham and along the main road to Allington. Her thick coat and her wool skirt kept her body warm, but her knees, exposed above the boots, were soon chilled. She felt quite giddy when they arrived at the cinema. Kevin put the bike in a nearby parking lot, securing it with a padlock and chain, then walked towards the cinema, leaving her to tag along behind. It was not as she had imagined, but she told herself that he was still shy. He paid for her, however, and bought her a bar of chocolate, airily waving aside her fumbling attempt to buy her own ticket, tall beside her because he was still wearing his helmet and had merely pulled a section of scarf away from his mouth to speak to the attendants.

The film terrified Marilyn. She liked films about pop stars or cowboys, or rich tycoons. At the most frightening bits she gripped the arms of her seat, the orange helmet resting on her lap, not liking to cling to Kevin.

He never touched her.

Afterwards he took her straight back to Framingham and dropped her at the station. He had scarcely spoken to her all the evening.

For Kevin, it was too early to go home. That man would still be there, with Jessie. He might even stay the night. At the thought, Kevin shuddered. He turned his bike towards the by-pass and cruised gently up Hatch Hill towards the house.

Marilyn sobbed as she walked across the railway bridge, past Fowler's Piece and the new estate, into Hawk's Row. She didn't know what she'd expected — a kiss, a cuddle, perhaps; certainly not two hours of terror and then the wordless dismissal. Luckily her parents would still be out at the pub; there would be no need for explanations. She let herself in with her key and went up to bed, where she cried herself to sleep.

CHAPTER
SIX

On Sunday morning Kevin stayed in bed until twelve o'clock. He'd stopped at the big house for hours the night before and had helped himself to some coffee cake he found in a tin. Then when he'd got home he'd finished the chocolate pudding Jessie and her fancy man had left; there was half a bowl of it. He wondered what they'd done together and imagined them, like in a film, drinking wine and snuggling up together. He'd kiss her and mess her about. From his sketchy experience, reinforced by what he'd seen on television and in the cinema, Kevin pictured Jessie's little mouth fixed to Bob's straight lips, her head pressed back, his hands wandering over her slight body. He saw, in memory, his mother, all those years ago. He'd watched them, her and the lodger, Len. Some lodger. One night Kevin had come downstairs and seen them on the rug in front of the fire. His mother had been making little sounds and he'd thought Len was hurting her; he'd run at him, hitting him with small fists and screaming.

Soon after, there'd been the fire, and his mother had gone. Now this other man would take Jessie away, unless he prevented it. When she called that lunch was ready, he went into the bathroom and ran himself a bath, lying in it till the water was cold, resisting the savoury smell of roasting lamb which floated up to him.

Jessie understood why Kevin was behaving so badly. Until she started going out with Bob, she'd always been available. But things were different now, and she must talk to him about it, make him understand.

At the thought of Bob, Jessie felt quite trembly. She could not believe that romance had come her way at last, for romance it was, though sedate, and one day they would be married.

Bob lived in a solid, four-bedroomed house in Nairn Road, on the other side of Allington. She could do it all up, change anything, he had said, but Jessie liked the things he and Valerie had gathered over the years. She'd add just a few of her own most valued possessions and any changes would be gradual. Nothing could happen until Kevin had made his plans. Jessie had thought of letting the house to him at a nominal rent, but it would make things too easy for him; he'd let off a couple of rooms himself and do no work, if she did, and end up in trouble through having time on his hands. She'd make a will, after she was married, leaving the house to him, and meanwhile, by letting it properly, she'd have some independence if she gave up working when Bob retired.

Married! Turning the oven down, hoping the potatoes would stay crisp until Kevin chose to appear, Jessie sighed like a young girl. So much would be transformed. But not yet: she need not face the challenge for a while.

Kevin appeared at last, his hair damp and slicked down; he'd probably finished her shampoo. Jessie carved him a generous portion from the leg of lamb. There was cauliflower to go with the roast potatoes, and onion sauce because he liked it. Kevin ate in silence, looking only at his plate.

"Did you enjoy the film?" Jessie tried, but he did not answer. After another few mouthfuls, she asked, "Was it raining when you got in?" Still no reply. "I'm going out to tea," she told him. She was going to meet Bob's sister, who lived in Clapham; Bob was picking her up at half-past two and she wouldn't be ready, at this rate. "I won't be late back," she added.

But why shouldn't she be? She need not answer to Kevin for her movements. The habit of years persisted, however, and his failure was her failure too; she must somehow win him round. Clearing the plates, dishing up the apple tart, Jessie remembered the fire that had killed her sister and saw again Len's desperate face.

"The boy did it, I know he did," Len had said. "I've caught him before, lighting matches."

But he'd said none of that to the police. It had been decided that the fire was caused by the paraffin stove flaring in a sudden draught. Kevin had admitted lighting it in the night; he'd woken and felt cold, and gone down for a warm while he ate a biscuit. He must have forgotten to turn it out when he went upstairs again, he'd said. It was lying on its side when the fire was finally extinguished, but it could have got knocked over in the confusion.

Whatever he'd done, he'd got away with it. While the house burned, he'd crawled from his bedroom window on to the flat roof of the shed, and was found there, cowering at the edge of it, by the firemen. He couldn't have meant to kill his mother, so what good would proving he'd been involved have done? Len disappeared when the funeral was over, and it was all a long time ago, but it was little wonder that Kevin had been difficult afterwards. As a small child he had been quiet but biddable, slow to make friends but happy alone with his mother. His father seldom appeared, and when he did, gave Kevin money to go to the cinema and later bought him a bicycle. Kevin looked like his father, a small, pale, agile man who could wriggle through the fanlights of windows and who finally carried a gun. Jessie never told Kevin that he'd died in prison.

Scraping his spoon against the plate, Kevin finished the apple tart, and Jessie washed up hurriedly. She was ready, in her green tweed coat and tan shoes, when Bob's car drew up outside, and ran out to join him before he could come to the house.

Kevin locked her out that night. He put the chain on the front door and bolted the back, and when she was forced to ring the bell, Kevin took no notice, the television on loud and a bottle of beer beside him. He'd been down to the pub earlier, and bought four pints. Bob, however, had not driven off. When he saw his betrothed apparently unable to get into her house, he was soon beside her on the step.

"Kevin must have locked up without thinking," Jessie said. "I don't want to make too much noise — the neighbours — " She rang the bell again and it could be heard echoing through the house.

Bob went round to the back and tried that door, but it

was secure. When he returned to the front, Kevin had drawn one of the curtains back and could be seen at the window, looking out at them, grimacing, a beer bottle in one hand.

"Come home with me and leave him to get on with it," said Bob. "The boy's been drinking."

"No — no, I couldn't do that," said Jessie, though walking away from her problems seemed a heavenly idea. "He'll give in." She pushed open the flap of the letter-box and called through, "Kevin, if you don't open the door I'll fetch the police."

Would she? Bob looked at her with puzzled admiration.

Nothing happened for several minutes. Then a light went on upstairs and Kevin's head poked out of the bathroom window.

"Silly cow. The back door was open all the time," he called.

It was unbolted now. Bob went in with Jessie. The television was still on in the living-room, and empty beer bottles lay on their sides on the carpet.

Jessie looked at Bob despairingly.

"He had some sweet ways as a child," she said.

Muriel and Howard also had roast lamb for lunch that Sunday, followed by blackberry and apple crumble. Afterwards, Howard suggested they should go for a walk while it was still fine, but Muriel said she had an important letter to write so he went alone. He saw it when he came back over an hour later, an airmail envelope on the hall table addressed to a William

Anderson, Esq., at an address in Perth, Australia.

"Who on earth is William Anderson?" he asked, when he had taken off his overcoat and tweed hat.

"He's old Mrs Anderson's son — the old lady at The Gables," said Muriel. "Billy, she calls him. He can't realize what a struggle she has to carry on up there, nor how much the house is worth. I'm sure, when he hears the facts, he'll persuade his mother to sell it."

"Do you think it's your business?" asked Howard.

"Yes, I do. If it was my mother, and I lived thousands of miles away, I'd be glad to hear about her," said Muriel.

As Muriel's mother had died fifteen years ago, the remark was pure hypothesis. But Howard knew when it was a waste of energy to try to get her to change her mind, so he said no more but went into the sitting-room, where he picked up the paper. Muriel would soon bring tea.

On Sundays, Mrs Anderson gave herself little treats. She had coffee for breakfast instead of tea, and she roasted a small joint, most weekends, a pound of topside or a piece of lamb. Then she could cut at it, cold, for a day or two, and turn any scraps into rissoles or shepherd's pie. She liked roast potatoes and would put one into the tin with the meat. There was never a feeling of extravagance with the Aga for the oven was always ready. Today, she had a half shoulder of lamb, the tastiest part, she always thought. She cored an apple to bake; the trees in the orchard had produced a fine crop this year and Joe Knox had picked them, leaving her several racks full in the shed and taking the rest for himself, an arrangement that suited them both.

Mrs Anderson enjoyed cooking. Domestic help was scarce after the war, and in the gaps between cooks, cook-generals and working housekeepers, she learned, by sheer experience, how to prepare appetizing dishes to tempt her ailing husband. After he died she gave up trying to find resident help. Now there were no one else's whims to consider, not even those of a casual guest. For years a girlhood friend who lived in London had paid visits. When Mrs Anderson still had the car they went for country drives. In return, Mrs Anderson had stayed at the flat in Kensington and the two widows went to theatres and to exhibitions. But Helen Combe had died seven years ago, and now Mrs Anderson had no friends left as old as herself.

When preparations for her lunch were made, Mrs Anderson settled down in the sitting-room with the church service on the radio, paying attention to it, not knitting or sewing. She had been brought up strictly in the Christian tradition and still hoped that she might be reunited with her sons and her husband in an after-life, although she expected to spend eternity divinely recycled in some way which might make recognition difficult. Until several years ago, she went to church regularly; then the by-pass had been built and the road she took to it was blocked by the new embankment. It was a long way now, on foot, unless you went over the fields. A new vicar had come soon after the by-pass had cut her off from the town, and once he had called on her. He had long, greasy, greying hair; wore a yellow shirt and green trousers; and did not look like a vicar at all. He had called Mrs Anderson ''dear'' and suggested she join the Darby and Joan Club. Mrs Anderson, daughter of a colonel and widow of a company chairman, gave him a chilling reply and never went near the church again, even on a fine day when the walk might not have been such an effort.

Latterly, she had wondered a little about the Darby and Joan Club. It would be nice to have a chat with someone who remembered Gallipoli. She noticed other old women, and an occasional man, when she went shopping, and there were the regular library users whom she knew quite well by sight, but in her day you did not talk to strangers: you waited to be introduced.

After her lunch, she dozed in her chair. Then she put on her coat, a woollen hood and her warm boots and walked round the garden. Its overgrown state worried her. Once, a full-time gardener, helped by a boy, had planted and cultivated, mowed and trimmed. Billy would soon set things to right, when he came back. But he hadn't come home even when his father died.

Such thoughts did no good. Mrs Anderson noticed buds forming here and there on spring-flowering shrubs; she broke off some spikes of forsythia to put in water. When they bloomed, it would make warm days seem nearer.

Back in the house, she played patience until it was time for tea, when she thought with pleasure of the coffee cake Muriel Dean had brought. She had eaten only small slices to make it last and it had certainly kept fresh. There should be about a third still left. She got out the tray and laid it with a cloth, the teapot, a cup and saucer, and put out the milk, then went to the tin.

It was empty.

Mrs Anderson stared at it in bewilderment, heart fluttering. She remembered seeing in the dustbin an empty spaghetti tin she couldn't recall opening; another time she had gone to the larder for a tin of beans and had found none when she was sure there were two or three. Once, when she thought she had several pounds in her purse, there had been only one. What did it mean? With shaking hands she replaced the empty cake tin in the larder. Had she finished it the day before after all? But no — she'd planned to spin the pleasure of it out over the weekend.

She must have eaten it, and forgotten: had tea twice over. True, she didn't remember but then old people often grew confused. For the first time in her life, Mrs Anderson began to fear that she might be losing her mind.

She forgot about her tea, sitting at the kitchen table, staring into space and making little mewing sounds of terror.

Nine-year-old Laura Finch spent that Sunday with her father. He drove up to the house to fetch her in his new Lancia and sped her to London, where he had a flat in Bayswater. During his marriage to Janet he had driven to London every day, despite the good train service, clocking up records for the journey and spending a lot on car park fees when he got there. Now, every other Sunday, he came to fetch Laura; sometimes it was a bind, but it was his right. Lately he had lapsed a little, and this time it was five weeks since he had seen his daughter.

Laura wore her new dark brown corduroy pinafore over a bottle green sweater, matching green tights, and her brown duffle coat. Her hair was dark and curly, like her mother's, held back by a ribbon snood to match her sweater. She waited by the window for him, and when the car drew up, Janet opened the door for her and let her run down the path, not coming out herself. She had nothing to say to Desmond.

Desmond gave Laura a hug that smelled of tobacco, and something else she could not identify. He belted her into the seat beside him. It was low, so she could not see out very well, since she was so small. He took corners at speed, and Laura, latched in a harness meant for an adult, lurched as he jerked the car roughly round them. Luckily most of the journey was along the motorway, but when they began to get held up in traffic, stopping and starting constantly, Laura suffered. She was pale green when they arrived at the flat.

''There's a surprise,'' Desmond said, and called, ''Pam, here we are.''

Laura, accustomed to spending the afternoon alone with her father watching television or playing card games — he had long abandoned taking her to museums or the zoo — after a restaurant lunch, noted, as she stood in the small hall, the smell of roasting meat, and as she started to undo her coat a woman came out of the kitchen.

''Well, here's Laura, Pam,'' said Desmond in what Laura thought of as a funny voice. ''You two'll get on fine, I know. This is Pam, Laura.''

''Hullo, Laura,'' said Pam. ''Of course we will.''

Laura looked at her solemnly, not speaking.

''Pam lives here now,'' said Desmond jollily. ''Let's all have a drink, shall we?''

''I must go to the bathroom,'' said Laura desperately, and fled.

Sounds of retching came to the ears of Pam and Desmond. Desmond shrugged.

''It's the car. She gets carsick,'' he said. ''She'll be all right in a minute. I need that drink.''

When Laura emerged from the bathroom, still pallid, her father and Pam were sitting on the sofa with large gins and tonics in their hands.

''Ah — better, then?'' said Desmond.

Laura nodded.

''We'll wait lunch for a bit, till you settle,'' said Pam, smiling. She was a short, plump woman, and looked, to Laura, quite old. She had cropped fair hair and wore a suede waistcoat and black trousers, with high-heeled shoes. There were bangles on both wrists and gold chains round her neck. She asked Laura a lot of questions about school but did not wait for any answers, making assumptions instead.

Lunch, when at last they ate it, was delicious — lamb, with redcurrant jelly. The pudding was apricot fool, with ice cream, and for tea there was chocolate cake. Laura, her nausea gone, ate heartily, and found there was no need to talk. Her father described the weather and the state of the traffic to Pam, and she related how she had gone to the corner shop, which opened on Sundays, for cream for the pudding, and described a red setter she'd met which was taking its owner for a walk.

Laura laughed at that. It was funny to think of a dog taking a person out. Then she bit back her laughter. It was disloyal to her mother to respond to this usurper, which in a confused way she felt Pam to be. There was only one bedroom in the flat; Laura had seen it many times. It held one large bed. Pam and her father must share it. It seemed funny. She wondered if they would have a baby, and when Pam cleared away the plates Laura stared with interest at her stomach, veiled as it was by the waistcoat. It did look quite round.

They played ludo after lunch, Pam yawning a little, and Laura noticed her rubbing her father's ankle with her foot. On the way back to Framingham, Laura was sick. Her father stopped the car and unbelted her just in time for her to reach the grass verge and lose the chocolate cake.

Janet spent Sunday morning giving the house a good clean and clearing out the kitchen cupboards. She hated it when Laura was with her father and always kept very busy then, trying not to think about them. She had just finished a late lunch of bread and cheese when there was a tap at the back door and Howard came into the kitchen. When he called, he always came straight in, not courting recognition on her doorstep.

"Howard, oh, how lovely," Janet cried. "What a lovely surprise!" In seconds she was in his arms. They clung together, his tweed coat rough against her face. He had never come round on a Sunday before.

Howard seemed to feel his heart literally expand as he held her; it was bliss to be so welcome. He had known that Laura was visiting her father and he was sure that he would find Janet alone. Because he had suggested to Muriel that they go for a walk together and she had refused, he felt no conscience qualm as he kissed Janet fervently.

But after a time she pushed him away.

"Howard, no," she said. "Let's go and sit down." She led the way towards the living-room. "Take off your coat," she added.

Howard obeyed, and then put his arms round her again. She was so slight: he could feel her ribs under her fluffy sweater. He slid his hands beneath it.

Janet melted against him briefly but then drew back.

"Not now, Howard," she said.

"Why not?" Howard murmured. She had the effect of making him feel not a day over thirty. "There's no one here."

"It might bring bad luck," Janet said, disentangling herself from his embrace.

"My darling, what do you mean?" asked Howard.

Janet loved to hear him utter endearments and the look she gave him now made him advance towards her, but she retreated.

"To Laura — some harm might come to her," she said. "Sit down, Howard — over there." She pointed to the sofa, at the same time sitting down herself in the one armchair.

"How could it?" Howard asked. He moved aside a patchwork pig Janet was making, some scraps of material, and her work-basket, so that he could do as she bid.

"Anything could happen when she's with Desmond," said Janet. "He's such a reckless driver. She always comes back pea-green. If we just took advantage of the opportunity to be happy together, the fates might make something dreadful happen. To punish us."

"But you aren't doing anything wrong," said Howard. "You aren't married any more." He was the adulterer.

"No, but I'd be enjoying myself. It might put her at risk," said Janet.

Howard saw that she meant it, in the manner of one who believes all nasty medicine must do good and all pleasure be a sin.

"Do you want me to go, then?" he asked.

"Oh no. Not if we can just chat," said Janet. "That would be perfect."

How illogical she was! Being happy chatting was allowed, but going to bed together was too risky. Howard smiled. He was always happy chatting to Janet and would store up small things to tell her on their Friday evenings together — some comic encounter in the underground or the latest problem in the uneasy love life of his junior partner, things that he thought would not interest Muriel, who anyway seldom had time to sit and listen.

She'd scarcely responded even when told that a series of meetings would make him late home on Fridays; he'd have something to eat in town, he'd said, so that she needn't keep a meal for him. Muriel, often at meetings herself, made no objection. It had been ridiculously easy. The only risk was that an acquaintance among his fellow commuters might notice him on his usual train and give him away. Howard now travelled at the rear of the train on Fridays, boarding late, and hung back at Framingham as the platform emptied before taking the footbridge to Fowler's Piece.

He spent nearly an hour with Janet that afternoon. Muriel had had her chance.

CHAPTER
SEVEN

Marilyn nearly didn't go to the coffee bar on Monday. She didn't want to risk seeing him after the misery of Saturday. She'd woken the next morning with a swollen face and reddened eyes, but her mother and father paid little attention, going off to the pub as usual, leaving her to cook the midday dinner: pork, it was, and she'd got the crackling lovely and crisp, but they didn't mention it. She'd timed it for when the pub closed, they wouldn't be back before, and had kept her head bent over her plate as she ate her own meal.

After she'd washed up and put everything away — Sunday was the only time the kitchen got a good clean-up, because she did it, sometimes even scrubbing the stone floor — she went up to her room and lay on her bed, mentally replaying the events of the previous evening. It was all her fault that it had gone so badly; she didn't get much practice at talking to boys. You couldn't count Joe Dent who swept the storeroom at the supermarket and helped to load the shelves; he'd just left school and was only a kid.

But if she didn't go to the coffee bar, there was nowhere else she fancied. She didn't want to go to one of the pubs; Wendy's or the Ingle Nook Café were too expensive and a bit fancy; if she bought sandwiches at Takeaway Snax, she'd have to eat them in the restroom at the store, and the other girls would be talking about their boyfriends or even their husbands; she could never join in with that sort of thing. So in the end she went, and he was there, sitting at a corner table with a plate of shepherd's pie. Marilyn collected her coffee and a ham-filled roll and walked towards another table.

"Hey — you — " He did not need to raise his voice, she was so aware of him. "Here," he said, waving his fork at the place opposite him. He'd left his gloves there, incredibly keeping the place for her, big black leather gauntlet gloves which she'd noticed on Saturday.

Marilyn spread a stiff smile across her face and bent to the business of unloading her tray. She moved his gloves to the end of the bench. Then she began to eat. She did not look at him, and she did not speak. Both chewed steadily, Kevin scraping his fork noisily across his plate to waste no morsel, Marilyn curling her tongue to hook wisps of lettuce and stray crumbs into her mouth. Then Kevin stood up.

"See you next Saturday," he said. "Quarter-past eight, same place," and was gone.

Mrs Anderson got up that Monday morning in a determined mood. She took pencil and paper to the larder, where she made a list of her stores. Later, when she opened a tin of peas to eat with her cold lamb, she crossed it off the list and put the new total, three tins of peas.

Next, she went down to the cellar and brought up a

bowl of hyacinth bulbs, just sprouting above their fibre. She put it on the kitchen window sill, so that the pale shoots would turn green and grow to the light. She moved slowly, tired today, checking everything that she did, stopping to look round and make sure she had closed the cellar door and even going back to it, to check again. She tested the bulb fibre for moisture and gave it some water. Then she wrote out her shopping list for the next day. She went into Framingham twice a week, and if she were tempted to skip Tuesday, always told herself that the weather might be worse by Thursday, or she not well. She needed to go to the bank and must buy bread, vegetables and fruit. She'd finished Oliver Cromwell and would get rid of him at the library. How many more months, years, would this go on: her regular days, carefully planned; the physical effort of toiling up the hill with her shopping? How long could she manage, if her mind was going? And why did she struggle on? What was the point?

I want to see Billy again, she told herself. He'll come back. I must manage. I must concentrate.

That night she slept better. The night before, she had lain in bed panicking that if she was really losing her memory, she'd be put into an asylum by someone like Muriel Dean. But on Tuesday her stores were as she had left them.

It was a grey day again, but there was no wind and the radio forecast rain. Mrs Anderson bought her groceries at Fresh Foods, paying the plain, fat girl.

"All right then, are you, love?" she always said as the last things were packed into the shopping basket.

Mrs Anderson did not care to be called "love" but she appreciated the kindliness and always said, "Yes, thank you, my dear." Marilyn knew her well by sight. Poor old thing, she would think, and would watch her totter from the shop if she wasn't already checking out another customer.

Mrs Anderson cashed her cheque and paid in her state pension, which came by post. She exchanged Oliver Cromwell for Disraeli, and took a book about Australia, too, illustrated in colour. Then she had her usual rest in the library, reading a magazine. At the greengrocer's she bought sprouts and a cauliflower, bananas, and, for a treat, some tangerines — or satsumas, as they were called nowadays. There were massed Christmas trees outside the shop, and fairy lights in the windows.

Footsteps came up behind her as she approached the turning from the High Street towards the by-pass. Hearing them, she drew her basket in to the side of the path to let whoever it was go past.

Kevin resisted the urge to give her a push and watch her tumble over, on his way back to Blewett's Garage with sandwiches from Takeaway Snax.

"Ta, Gran," he said. "Be seeing you."

That evening, Bob and Jessie sat in armchairs on opposite sides of the fireplace, where a log fire burned, in the sitting-room of his house in Nairn Road. Bob's daily housekeeper had left dinner for two prepared — a casserole in a low oven, and mince pies. Jessie was still worrying about Kevin's conduct on Sunday evening but Bob told her he'd get over his upset and that anyway she mustn't let it distress her.

"It will all sort itself out," Bob said, determined that it should.

When he took her home, a light in an upstairs window showed that Kevin was already there and in bed. The door was on the Yale, so he'd thought better of a repetition. Bob came in and stayed for a little while. Later, when Jessie went into the bathroom, there was a little heap of singed, charred undergarments in the bath, two pairs of her panties, a bra, some tights, the nylon fabric partly dissolved. Jessie almost gave a little scream at the sight of them. In that instant, her long uncertainty was resolved and she knew that Kevin had started the fire that killed his mother. Now he was threatening her.

CHAPTER
EIGHT

Marilyn's mood soared and plummeted all the week. Kevin did not go to the coffee bar again. When Saturday came she walked to work thinking that as last week had been such a failure, she'd stand him up; she hadn't promised to meet him, he'd just taken it for granted. She forgot about it in the shop, kept busy with the Saturday crowd, but by the evening she'd changed her mind again. If she didn't go out with him, what would she do? Stop at home, alone, with the television? She'd tried discos on her own and that had been no fun. He was just shy; she'd have to make more of an effort, that was all.

Her mother and father had already left for the pub when she got home. The frying pan, the fat in it still warm, was where her mother always left it, on the stove ready for use. Marilyn fried herself two eggs and some chips; she'd felt very hungry the week before; the chocolate Kevin had bought her hadn't kept her going long. There was some fruit cake in a tin and she took a slice of that upstairs, to eat while she got ready. There wasn't much time. She had a bath with foaming oil which she'd bought when it was on offer at the toiletry counter, and dressed in a new wool skirt, gathered into a band round her thick waist and patterned with little rosebuds on a black background. She had a black sweater to go with it, and a cornelian pendant on a silver chain as an ornament. With the hood of her checked coat pulled up against the rain that was falling, she set off for the station.

He was already there, his bike parked outside the booking hall. The white scarf was pulled across his face and he wore his helmet. He gave her the orange one as she went to meet him.

"Get on," he said, as brusquely as the week before. It was his late week at the garage and he had come straight from work. As soon as she was mounted behind him, he sped off, but this time, when they reached Allington, he turned away from the brightly lit centre of the town, where the shops and the cinema were, and drove out into a residential area. The tyres splashed on the wet road.

"Where are we going?" Marilyn asked, but if he heard, he did not answer.

After making several turns, they stopped outside a semi-detached house in a quiet road. It was dimly lit by street lights; there were a few cars parked here and there against the kerb, but no one walking their dog, or hurrying home: no sign of life, in fact. Kevin told Marilyn to get off the bike.

"Where are we?" she asked.

"I live here," said Kevin.

He must be taking her to meet his parents! Marilyn followed him as he pushed the bike up the path. There was a shed at the back, and he wheeled it inside, carefully hoisting it on to its stand and leaving it with a lingering glance.

"Come on," he said, and walked round to the front door which he opened with a key from his pocket. The house was in darkness.

"My aunt's out," said Kevin. "She's got this feller." Still wearing his coat and helmet, he went into the living-room. Marilyn followed.

"You live with your aunt?" she asked.

"Yes. My mum's dead — I'm an orphan," said Kevin.

"Oh — that's awful! Poor — " but she didn't know what to call him. "I don't know your name," she said.

"Kevin. Kevin Timms," he said.

"Mine's Marilyn Green," she said eagerly, and felt easier now that they were introduced, as it were.

The living-room was furnished with comfortable chairs and a small sofa upholstered in rust-coloured fabric. Kevin lit the gas fire; then he pushed past her and went out of the room. Marilyn heard him going upstairs. She laid the orange crash helmet on a small table beneath the window and wondered if she should take off her wet coat. Anxiety, as much as cold, made her shiver, and she kept it on. Kevin soon returned; he had taken off his jacket and helmet, and the scarf, and had slicked back his hair. He wore canvas shoes instead of his boots, and he carried four pint bottles of beer which he put down on the floor in front of the sofa; then he went into the kitchen and returned with two glasses. He switched on the television, handed Marilyn a glass of beer and poured one for himself, which he drained straight off. He refilled the glass.

"Sit down, girl," he said, sitting on the sofa and

patting the place beside him. The colour came up on the television and tanks were revealed, guns blazing into distant hills, with American soldiers crawling behind them with twigs tucked into camouflage nets on their helmets.

Careful not to spill her beer, Marilyn sat down on the edge of the sofa. She took a sip of beer and tried not to pull a face. She didn't like the smell of it; her father came home every night exuding beery fumes.

"Much better than the cinema, this. Cosier, like," said Kevin. He was no good at soft talk, and saw little point in it. He emptied his glass again and refilled it. "Sit back, relax," he said.

Marilyn moved so that she leaned against the sofa. The room was warming up, and she unbuttoned her coat. Kevin sprawled beside her and put an arm along the back of the sofa, behind her. The hood of her coat separated her neck from his arm. They sat staring at the screen. Guns fired and there were cries as men fell wounded. Kevin negotiated the barrier of her coat's hood and tangled his hand in Marilyn's hair, then pulled it. It hurt, and she squealed, "Oh, don't." He let go then, and slid his fingers inside her sweater at the back of her neck, rubbing it where he could feel a knob at the top of her spine. At first she sat stiffly, apprehensive, but after a while she began to like the sensation and relaxed against his hand. At once, he took it away, finished his beer and opened another bottle.

Marilyn kept her gaze turned towards the television screen. Planes were diving now on the combatant troops. Men's bodies were blown into the air and screams could be heard. Kevin moved closer to her, pressing his leg in its faded jeans against the fabric of her skirt where her coat lay open over her plump thigh. She moved her leg away but he moved closer, pressing against her, his hand at her neck again. When no more happened, she relaxed once more, and again he released her to drink. Then, without further warning, she felt hard lips on her mouth and a hand thrusting up her skirt. His thin body moved on top of her and pressed her against the sofa. He smelled sweaty. Marilyn was very frightened; she held herself rigid but did not resist: this was experience; this was what other girls talked and giggled about and now it was happening to her. But then she felt his hand jerking at her clothes and his naked finger prying, trying to get between her tightly closed legs. She reacted instinctively. She was bigger than he was, and she pushed him away, hitting wildly at him with her handbag which had lain on the sofa beside her.

''No, no!'' she cried, and because her resistance surprised him, she managed to thrust him off, get to her feet and rush into the hall, where she stared round for a moment in panic, then wrenched open the front door and fled down the path. The door banged shut behind her, and by the time Kevin had opened it to go after her, she was running along the road.

He went back into the living-room and finished the beer. On the television screen, bullets whistled past soldiers' heads and a helicopter hovered; he stared at the mock war, not registering what he was looking at, and he was filled with bitter fury. Deliberately, he allowed his rage to boil.

Not long after Marilyn had run away, Kevin finished the beer. Then he fetched his coat, his scarf, his gloves and his helmet, and got on his bike again.

Too scared and too short of breath to sob, Marilyn ran towards the town centre. It hadn't taken long on the bike, but now it seemed a great way off and she was not sure if she was taking the right turnings. When she realized that Kevin was not following she slowed down to a walk. It was still raining. At last the street lights grew brighter and soon she came into the familiar shopping area. She had no idea of the time; it felt as though hours had passed since she left home, and the last bus for Framingham might have gone, but as she reached the bus station one was just pulling out. It stopped in answer to her signal and she got on, sitting in a front seat behind the driver.

The journey home took some time as the bus wandered through various villages on the way; there were very few passengers. Marilyn sat there, weeping, until the bus stopped at the station where Kevin had met her so recently. Snuffling into a handkerchief, she crossed the railway bridge and walked past Fowler's Piece to Hawk's Row. There was no one about to witness her distress as she reached her own house at last.

Her parents were still out. Fumbling for her key in her bag, she did not hear the figure that came up behind her on rubber-soled feet. Marilyn felt a hard shove in her back as she opened the door. She was pushed over her own threshold and her arm was seized and twisted up behind her back as the front door banged. A hand went over her mouth and she was dragged through the hall towards the kitchen at the back of the house. She could hear her attacker breathing hard as he fumbled to turn on the light. Only then did Marilyn realize who it was. Kevin had called at the Brewer's Arms, and fired with whisky on top of the beer he had drunk, had roared off to Framingham for revenge, passing the bus on the way. He had enough wits left to realize that she might be on it, so he hurried ahead and parked the bike against the kerb where Hawk's Row began. He did not know which was Marilyn's house, so he hid in a gateway on the opposite side of the road to wait for her. He heard her dragging footsteps and her snuffles minutes before he saw her.

Marilyn was too frightened to scream. Kevin hauled her into the kitchen and hit her hard on the face with the back of his hand in its leather glove, and as she reeled across the room he came at her again, slapping her first on one cheek and then the other.

"Cow, bitch," he yelled at her, and with obscenities pouring from him, caught her by the hair and gave her a great push which sent her staggering against the draining board. Crockery piled there crashed over, and Marilyn put her hands out in front of her to fend him off.

"Don't, don't," she wailed, but he brought his knee up and kicked her in the stomach. She doubled up, gasping, and he took hold of her again by her hair and flung her across the room. She slithered to the ground, pulling a chair over as she fell on to the dirty stone floor. Kevin stood over her, kicking her, still cursing. Her thick coat protected her to some extent and she went on struggling, trying to get up. Then Kevin leaned down, took hold of her coat at the neck and banged her head hard against the floor. She gave a little moaning cry and he cursed her again, raised her head and began thumping it on the floor, again and again, using all his force, until at last he realized that she had ceased to resist.

"Christ!" Kevin stared at her. He lifted her shoulders and shook her, but her head fell back and she hung there heavy in his grasp, a dead weight. Then he saw the blood.

He let her go and her head thumped to the floor once more as he sprang away from her, away from the blood that came from her ears and from the back of her head where the skin had split.

She was dead! The fat cow had died on him! But it wasn't his fault — he hadn't meant her to die! He'd only intended to teach her a lesson.

Vomit rose in Kevin's throat and he lurched to the sink where he retched up the liquor he had drunk, shuddering. It wasn't fair. Things always went wrong for him.

He became calmer as his head cleared. There was a way out, the same one he always used in trouble. He looked around at the chaos in the room — plates broken on the floor, a chair knocked over and the draining board stacked with dirty crockery and cutlery. There was a pan with some fat in it on the stove. Kevin took off a glove and felt in his pocket for his matches. With his gloved hand he turned the gas burner right up under the pan of fat and lit it, replacing the spent match in the box. While he was waiting for the fat to heat, he saw a bottle of cooking oil on the dresser. There was only a little left in it, but he poured it over Marilyn, standing well away from her to avoid the blood which made a pool round her head. It didn't take long for the fat in the pan to ignite: there was a plop and a burst of flame. It would seem more like an accident if it fell off the stove and the blazing fat poured over the girl. People would think she'd slipped and knocked the pan over. It was too hot for him to get near it now, and there was all that blood on the floor. He picked up a chair and threw it at the stove, then jumped backwards as the pan fell and the fire swooshed towards him. There wouldn't be much left of her. No one would know what had happened.

He shut the kitchen door, then let himself cautiously out at the front. It was still raining, and there was still no one about as he ran up the road, his face masked by his white scarf and his helmet on. He saw no one as he retrieved the bike, started it up, and roared away.

She hadn't known his name until tonight.

Kevin went back over the railway bridge to the station and then, instead of turning off for Allington, swung the other way towards the by-pass. In a few minutes he was going up Hatch Hill, faster than usual, forgetting to throttle back and approach quietly. But he slowed down before he reached the gateway of The Gables and turned in, his lights picking up the dripping laurels and other shrubs bordering the drive. It was still raining. He hid the machine in the bushes as usual, then walked up to the house and along the path round to the window he always used. No lights showed upstairs. He was clumsy tonight, and the window made a faint squeak as he eased it up, but, so far away in her room, the old woman would never hear it.

He took off his canvas shoes, which were soaking, and stood them on the dustsheet that covered the dining-room floor. He'd had a good investigation in here, finding the table and twelve chairs under covers, and a big sideboard, but there was nothing in any of the cupboards except some funny old bottles with glass stoppers, empty. He'd had a sniff at one, and it smelled a little musty. There were some felt table mats in a drawer; that was all.

Tonight he went quickly up to his attic room, turned on the fire, and lay on the bed in the darkness, gradually letting the realization of what had happened come over him.

The stupid bitch must have had a rotten thin skull if she couldn't stand up to a few thumps. It wasn't his fault that she'd snuffed it, and he didn't mean to take the blame. He began to shiver, and soon the shivering turned into frightened sobbing not unlike Marilyn's as she made her lonely way home. After a while, his sobs lessened and he began to think more calmly. By now the house would be blazing and no one would realize that someone had been in there with Marilyn. The television was always warning about frying pans catching alight; that was what had given him the idea, though such accidents never happened in Jessie's well-run kitchen. As he thought of his aunt, a hollow sensation filled him: what would happen to him? Who would look after him?

For the first time, his sanctuary at The Gables failed to soothe him; he soon went home, and to bed, forgetting about the beer bottles, the glasses and the orange crash helmet left in Jessie's living-room.

The next day he offered to peel the potatoes for lunch and cleaned all the windows, as it was fine. Filled with disquiet at these unlikely actions, Jessie didn't mention the mess she had found when she got home the night before: the unwashed glasses and the empty bottles. She took the orange helmet up to his room while he was busy in the kitchen and put it on the top shelf in his wardrobe, and she asked no questions about his evening.

Kevin had found bloodstains on his canvas shoes. He wrapped them in newspaper and put them in the wardrobe; he'd ditch them sometime when he went out. He had a second pair with some wear left in them. He did not notice a smear of blood on his white scarf, but he saw that the fringed ends were scorched where they had caught the flames from the gas. He shoved it into the bottom drawer of his chest of drawers, under a sweater.

It was getting on for midnight when Marilyn's parents tacked homewards along Hawk's Row. Fred Green had once worked as a storekeeper in a warehouse near Allington, but now he was unemployed; he had fallen from a ladder at work three years ago, breaking his hip and cracking his spine, and was off sick for months. When he recovered, he could no longer do the same job, which involved a lot of fetching and carrying as well as ladder-climbing. He was offered a post as a sweeper in the warehouse, but soon declared that all the standing made his leg ache and gave it up; since then he had developed a taste for leisure, and had managed to avoid finding work he could do, drawing state benefit instead of wages. He spent his mornings studying racing form and his afternoons at the betting shop, with a midday interlude at one pub or another, though the Jockey and Groom was his favourite.

Ena Green worked in the kitchen at the Rose and Crown, preparing vegetables and washing up, and occasionally making simple dishes. Her labours there gave her no interest in cleaning her own house and she washed up at home only when there weren't any plates or cutlery left to use. She had her mid-day meal at the Rose and Crown and took home food she scavenged every day: pies, pastries, cooked meat. Fred had a snack at the pub for his lunch, and whatever she brought back in the evening; sometimes there was enough for Marilyn too, but if not there was usually bacon in the larder, and eggs in a box on the dresser. The Greens had no refrigerator.

Since his accident, Fred had got rather thin and walked with a limp; Ena was plump and red-faced. Neither took much notice of Marilyn; she was a docile girl who gave no trouble and did as she was told, contributing a good portion of her wages to the household budget. She did the shopping, buying from Ena's list during one of her breaks at work. It was easy for her, with everything on hand in the supermarket.

When Marilyn was born, her parents had named her optimistically, expecting her to grow up into a golden girl, but when she didn't, they gradually lost interest, talking round her, treating her as if she were some rather unwelcome household pet, a dog, perhaps, whom for some reason they had to house but preferred to ignore. They had no idea that she had a date that evening.

When they reached the front door, her key was in it.

Swaying a bit, Fred turned it.

"Silly girl, asking for trouble," he muttered, but he was in a good mood as he'd had a winner that afternoon and they'd enjoyed themselves at the pub. He opened the door and they went into the hall. The light was on. Ena sniffed.

"What has she been doing?" she said. "Burning the kitchen down?" She went unsteadily to the door and opened it. Smoke eddied towards them.

"Must have left the oven on," said Fred. "Here, let me." He pushed past Ena and lumbered into the kitchen, aiming for the window, which he opened, coughing. Then he turned to the stove where one burner was alight, and turned it out. The top of the stove was blackened.

"What a mess," said Ena, behind him.

"The floor's slippery," said Fred. "Be careful. I'll open the back door to get rid of this smoke."

Then he saw her, lying on the floor, face turned to one side, the blood all around her.

Police Constable Frewen answered the call to Hawk's Row. He was travelling along Framingham by-pass when he got it, the nearest car to the incident, on the look-out for drunks and other Saturday night troubles.

While Ena was making the emergency call from a telephone box, Fred had gone upstairs and fetched the quilt from Marilyn's bed to cover her legs and make her look more seemly. Then he sat beside her, holding her limp, gloved hand, much too late, and waited for the police.

Ena, returning, rallied and thought tea would help to pull them round. Though blackened and scorched, the burner had been alight when they came in so it must be working. She lit a different one and put the kettle on, and had just got cups and the pot ready, rinsing them at the sink from among those waiting to be washed, when Frewen arrived. She ran plenty of water, hot from the geyser, noticing no smell of vomit.

Frewen had seen some surprising things in his time in the force, but he had never yet seen a mother brewing tea literally over the corpse of her daughter. The message to go to Hawk's Row had mentioned an accident, and the ambulance had been sent for too, but Frewen had not expected a fatality. He could see at once that the girl was dead although a doctor would have to pronounce that this, in fact, was so.

''Both of you — out of here, please,'' he said curtly, and then, realizing that shock took strange forms, added more gently, ''Come along, please.''

In the living-room, piles of newspapers had to be moved from the chairs, and a dirty plate and cup from the sofa, whose stuffing was bursting out of rents in the back and sides, before anyone could sit down. Frewen shut the couple in, then went back to the kitchen and gingerly turned off the gas, using the tips of his fingers protected by a handkerchief. He looked down at the girl and observed the woollen glove on the hand the father had been holding, and he saw the blood, congealed now, around her head. A scorched frying pan lay upside down on the floor, and, in a corner where it had rolled, an empty cooking-oil bottle, the hinged lid open.

Then he went out to the car to report his findings and ask for help.

He returned to the parents after that, and while waiting for his superiors to arrive, asked them exactly what had happened and began to write it down. Before they had told him much, the ambulance arrived.

CHAPTER
NINE

An Incident Room was set up during the night, when it was seen that Marilyn Green had been the victim of a violent assault ending in death. Detective Chief Inspector Sprockett, head of Allington CID, was in charge, responsible to Detective Chief Superintendent Winslow, head of the division. However, it was Detective Sergeant Crisp and a constable who arrived first at Hawk's Row, in response to Frewen's summons.

Marilyn had not been dead long. She was still warm. The doctor, when he came, said in his cagey way that he would be more precise after the post-mortem, but it seemed safe to say the cause of death was likely to be a fractured skull.

By the time road blocks were set up in an effort to trap the killer, Kevin was at home and in bed.

The parents — one or both of them — could have killed the girl. Such things happened. There was blood on the father's clothing. It was obvious that both had been drinking; in a fit of rage, the father might have set about his daughter. They were brought to Allington Central police station to make statements; witnesses would be found to confirm when they left the pub and this could be related to the time of death, when the doctor gave his opinion.

The fire was probably an accident due to the struggle that had clearly taken place, but Frewen, in his report, had mentioned the upturned, empty cooking-oil bottle. It would be tested for prints, though neither Sprockett nor Crisp had much hope that any other than those of the Greens would be found.

Fred Green's vigil beside the dead girl, while Ena went to the telephone box to call the police, could have been due to remorse, or simply an act to account for the blood that Marilyn's attacker might have on his clothes. But a boyfriend was the likely answer.

"Her keys were in the door," Crisp said. "Funny, that. Left for someone following her to let himself in?"

The parents insisted that they did not know if Marilyn had a date that night; they did not think she knew any boys. The post-mortem might indicate otherwise, and Marilyn's workmates might know more than her parents about how she spent her leisure time. Crisp roused the manager of Fresh Foods to find out what he could tell them. They went together to the shop, to obtain the names and addresses of the staff, so that they could be questioned without delay.

It was a busy night for the Allington force, with the forensic team working at the dead girl's home. Door-to-door inquiries would begin in the neighbourhood in the morning.

Someone, somewhere, might have heard or seen something.

* * *

Janet was rolling out the pastry for an apple pie when the doorbell rang on Sunday morning. A uniformed policeman stood outside. He told her that he was inquiring into an accident in Hawk's Row the previous night and wondered if she had heard or seen anything unusual.

Janet had not. She had listened to records while she did some sewing and had gone to bed at half-past ten.

The policeman asked if there was anyone else in the house who might have noticed something.

"There's my daughter. She's only nine," said Janet. "She was in bed by half-past eight."

Laura wanted to know why the constable had called, and Janet told her, making light of it.

"I heard a motor-bike," said Laura. "I woke up once and it went by." She'd been dreaming she was with her father and Pam, hurtling along a switchback road in the Lancia, and had woken in terror, to hear the ordinary sound of the motor-bike, going rather fast.

"Well, that's normal," said Janet. "Motor-bikes do go by, don't they?"

That afternoon, Laura's friend Jenny came to tea, and when her mother collected her later, she told Janet that a girl had died in Hawk's Row and it was rumoured that the house had been broken into.

Janet wondered briefly if she should tell the police about the motor-bike Laura had heard, since a serious crime seemed to have occurred, but decided that someone else must have heard it too, and so it need not concern them. She forgot about it.

* * *

The manager of Fresh Foods, questioned in the small hours of Sunday morning, had not been able to give the police any help about Marilyn's private life. She was a quiet girl who kept herself to herself, and a good worker.

"Had she a boyfriend?" Detective Sergeant Crisp had asked.

"Not that I know of," the manager had said. "Better ask the girls."

But the girls who worked in the shop gave the same answer. Of all the staff, Joe Dent, who swept the floors, washed the counters and helped unload the goods, was the most distressed. Marilyn had always been pleasant to him and would give him a hand with a heavy case if she was passing and saw him struggling. He couldn't get over the fact that he had talked to her on Saturday, and now she was dead. Sandra had snuffled into a handkerchief, shocked by the news and sorry, now that it was too late, that she hadn't been nicer to Marilyn. Rene said bluntly that she'd always been a quiet one and those were the ones who knew it all.

On Monday, soon after the supermarket opened, Crisp and Detective Constable Mitchell went there to see if any of them had remembered something that might throw light on the dead girl's movements and possible contacts, but no one could add to what had already been said.

"Dinner time — where did she go? Eat her lunch with the rest of you?" Crisp asked.

He learned that Marilyn had gone to the coffee bar every day; extravagant, it was, Rene said, when the others ate sandwiches in the restroom.

Crisp and Mitchell went straight to the coffee bar, which they found still closed so early in the day. They waited for it to open, their car parked on a yellow line, discussing the post-mortem report which had confirmed the cause of death as a fractured skull. Marilyn had other injuries: severe bruising on the body and on the face, indicating a savage attack; someone had put the boot in, though in fact he was probably wearing canvas shoes since the prints on the dirty kitchen floor showed the ridged rubber soles of sneakers. There was one distinct one; the rest were blurred by the parent Greens tramping about when they found the girl. This, and an alien fingerprint found on the cooking oil bottle, was proof that there had been an intruder and that the parents were not involved.

"Could have been someone picked her up that evening," Mitchell volunteered.

"May not even have done that. May have followed her home," said Crisp. "Some lad hanging about with nothing to do but look for trouble."

There had been a folk evening in Framingham Community Hall on Saturday night, but the dead girl had not been among the young people there. So far no one had been found who had seen her. A few known villains had been interviewed and all had accounted for their movements at the relevant time. Because no obvious suspect had surfaced right away, Crisp had the feeling they might be in for a long hunt.

"Sad sort of girl, really," said Mitchell. "No friends, and that."

"Poor bloody bitch," said Crisp. "Come on, let's get

moving. They're opening up.''

A husband and wife ran the coffee bar. Crisp showed them the only photograph of Marilyn that her parents could produce; it was taken while she was still at school, in white shirt and striped tie.

The woman said she was always in the kitchen making the hot orders and never had time to notice the customers; they were mostly young workers from nearby shops and offices, for this was the trade they aimed at.

''She had one of those blanket-type coats,'' Crisp said. ''Green and orange checks, with a hood. Distinctive.''

''Plenty of girls have those coats these days,'' said the woman.

''Look — those kids are just hands taking the plates and paying,'' said the man. ''I don't take a lot of notice of them. But that coat — yes — I reckon I have seen that girl. She came in most days.''

He could tell them nothing about her, however — whether she came with a friend or met anyone.

''Take it or leave it, eh?'' said Crisp, as he and Mitchell returned to the car. ''Chummy seems to have been the only one to take any notice of her. We'll come back later and see if any of the regulars can help.''

At twelve o'clock the two policemen took a seat at a table near the door, with tea and sandwiches. As various girls and youths came in, Crisp showed them the photograph. Some of them said they recognized Marilyn, but no one knew anything about her. No one had spoken to her. She might have met a fellow, or she mightn't, was the general opinion; no one would have bothered either way.

Kevin never went to the coffee bar again. That Monday he bought sandwiches at Takeaway Snax, wearing a new blue scarf which he had taken the night before from the cloakroom at The Gables. It was soft wool, and warm. The old girl wouldn't miss it, or if she did, she'd think she'd lost it somewhere.

He'd dumped his bloodstained sneakers, in their newspaper wrapping, in the dustbin at The Gables.

CHAPTER
TEN

Mrs Anderson received few personal letters these days. Her mail was mostly circulars, company reports from her husband's firm, and her pension cheques. Occasionally a niece of her husband's wrote to her from the Isle of Man. On Monday morning, however, a blue airmail envelope lay on the mat. Heavy black scribbles marked it. Mrs Anderson took it into the sitting-room and slit it open with a paperknife. She took out the letter and glanced at the heading and then, without reading it, replaced it, opened a drawer of her desk and put it inside. After that she stood at the window looking at the wintry garden for quite ten minutes before she was able to get on with her morning tasks. She had slept badly the night before, imagining, as she lay wakeful, that she heard noises in the house. She checked her stores with the list in the larder and it tallied.

On Tuesday, she went shopping as usual. A cold wind caught at her as she walked towards the subway. Her hat was well skewered on, but her coat blew away from her thin legs and she was glad of her warm boots, though they were tiring to walk in. At the library she changed Disraeli for Earl Haig. In that earlier war she had become a VAD nurse after her father died from wounds received at Mons. Her brother was killed in the Dardanelles and few of the young men she had known in her girlhood survived. She had met her husband while she was nursing; he was wounded on the Somme. More and more often, Mrs Anderson found her thoughts returning to those days, and the years after the first war when the machinery of daily existence had been something one took for granted, and there were maids to cook and clean. Today, everything was a struggle; it would be easy to lapse into squalor, to grow careless about washing and using clean linen. She had strict rules and a timetable to keep her life orderly; but now, with her strange forgetfulness, she was afraid that she was not succeeding in warding off disintegration. She must try harder, she resolved, sitting in the library reading the *Guardian*. No paper had been delivered to The Gables that morning and Mrs Anderson liked to check on her shares. For years she had regularly attended the shareholders' meetings, but now the struggle of crossing London to the City where they were held was too much. She'd given up her London dentist, too, and when she last had a twinge had gone to a young man in Framingham who was very kind but whose lavender overall and tank of tropical fish had amazed her as much as the new-fangled chair that had swung her into a horizontal position. She had three teeth on a plate; the rest were her own. She would not accept the young dentist's suggestion that she should come twice a year for inspection, preferring to wait until pain struck. She passed the dentist's surgery on the way from the library to Fresh Foods; a patient stood on the step, waiting for admittance. Mrs Anderson pushed on and parked her shopping basket near the supermarket checkout. She shopped methodically, consulting her list, leaning on the wire trolley for an unobtrusive rest.

The helpful, fat girl was not at any of the tills. One was in the charge of a florid-faced woman with black curls whom Mrs Anderson found intimidating, and at the other was a girl Mrs Anderson had never seen before.

Mrs Anderson went to the wiry-haired woman. Perhaps the plain girl was ill.

Pushing away up the road, Mrs Anderson noticed the legs of passers-by and not their faces, anxious to avoid a collision on the pavement. She did not recognize ankles, and was surprised when hailed.

"Mrs Anderson! Out shopping again? Would you like a lift home?"

Muriel Dean was walking towards her.

"Oh!" It seemed the most wonderful suggestion. "Thank you — but I haven't quite finished my shopping," said Mrs Anderson.

"Well, I'll be a few minutes, and I've got to get some petrol," said Muriel. "Take your time. I'll meet you at Blewett's Garage. I can wait there on the forecourt, till you come."

Mrs Anderson hastened to the greengrocer's; she seemed to be eating more bananas than usual. When she reached the garage, Muriel's car was being filled up by a short, thin youth with a bright blue woollen scarf wound round his neck. Mrs Anderson paid no attention to him as Muriel helped her into the car and put away her shopping.

Dropping her at The Gables, Muriel said, ''We'll be alone for Christmas this year, Howard and I. Our daughters can't get home. Won't you help us eat our turkey? We'll have it in the middle of the day. I'll come and fetch you. Now, I won't let you say no. I'm sure you haven't already accepted another invitation and that you'll be on your own. So you can't refuse.''

I can telephone and make some excuse, Mrs Anderson thought, when she had gone; and then, a little later, I'd better get her a present.

Would anyone have seen Marilyn on his bike? Kevin fretted about it at intervals. That coat of hers was something people would remember, but he'd been well muffled in his scarf, and when they went to the cinema he'd kept his helmet on until they were in their seats. No one could put the finger on him, even if she'd been noticed with a bloke. He'd deny ever having seen her, if anyone asked. The fuzz might come nosing round. But then, if the house had burnt to the ground like that other time, there'd be no mystery, nothing to ask about. No one had said anything about a bad fire in Framingham. He'd have liked to have gone past to look at it, gaze on the smoking ruins, but that would be asking for it. Coppers had nothing better to do than ask silly questions about where's your insurance.

He worked with more application than usual in the days that followed, so that Dave Blewett began to hope that something might be made of him after all; he'd been thinking of giving him the sack for his lack of enthusiasm and surly ways, and if he was to do it, it would have to be soon or the boy could go to the courts pleading wrongful dismissal. Dave sighed at a world which made skiving easy and penalized the industrious.

Kevin got a kick out of seeing Mrs Anderson getting into Muriel's car. He knew Muriel by sight as she was a regular customer but he didn't know her name. He never bothered with names; he didn't know Mrs Anderson's.

The inquest on Marilyn was held on Wednesday morning, and, after formal evidence of identification, was adjourned pending further inquiries. A reporter from the local weekly paper went back to the office to write up his story. *Girl perishes in mystery blaze*, he thought, would be good, but it seemed to have been more a smoulder than an inferno.

So close to Christmas, the shops were crowded when Mrs Anderson went into Framingham on Thursday. She bought extra supplies to last over the festival weekend, and had ordered two dozen eggs from the milkman, who would not come on Sunday, Christmas Day or Boxing Day. Seldom indecisive in her life, she was now, about Muriel's invitation. Thinking it over, she had concluded that it would be rather a treat to go out, but she had been apart from society for so long that she feared the effort of making conversation and generally being a good guest would be a severe strain. She would make up her mind at the last moment, she resolved, taking a chicken from the cool shelf at Fresh Foods in case she stayed at home. But she must buy some suitable gift, in case she went.

Soap, she thought, and headed for the chemist's, passing Pandora on the way. She paused. Why not have a look here, first? She had never been inside. Mrs Anderson went in, dragging her shopping basket; it was a nuisance in crowded places, bumping into other customers and taking up a lot of space. Pandora's was crammed with people buying last-minute presents. Hovering on the fringe of them, too small, and too encumbered by the basket to see past them to the wares on offer, Mrs Anderson felt a tug at her sleeve and saw a small girl with dark curly hair and large brown eyes looking at her.

"Can I help you?" she asked, with an air of importance.

Mrs Anderson looked at the child in surprise. She seemed rather young to be an assistant.

"Laura — oh, there you are," came another voice, and a dark young woman, whom the child closely resembled, clove a way towards them through the customers.

"I'm helping this lady," said Laura.

"Well — " Janet looked at Mrs Anderson. "Laura does know where everything is, and could tell you the price," she said. "I'm afraid it's difficult to see things, we're so busy. There's a chair at the back. Would you like to sit down and tell Laura what you want to see? She'll bring things then, to show you. And let me take that." She held out a hand for the basket. "I'll put it at the back too, it'll be quite safe there."

Mrs Anderson found the thought of a chair attractive. So few shops had them now. "Thank you," she said.

People were really very kind.

"Come with me," said Laura, and pulling the old lady's sleeve, led her through the shop to where, in a recess near the till, was an upright wooden chair. Mrs Anderson sat down gladly, and told Laura she wanted a present for someone quite a lot older than her mother, but not nearly as old as Mrs Anderson.

"What price?" asked Laura practically.

"Oh — " Mrs Anderson wondered what would be appropriate. "Two pounds?" she said. "Or three?"

Laura disappeared into the mob, and while she was gone, Mrs Anderson watched the dark girl and another woman with neat white hair cut in a bob wrapping parcels and taking money. Trade was non-stop. Soon Laura reappeared with a patchwork oven glove, a matchbox in a painted case, a patchwork pin cushion and a patchwork tea cosy, and some lavender bags made of muslin. Mrs Anderson chose the lavender bags, because she had made them herself, long ago, using lavender from the garden, and the pin cushion.

Laura took the money and wrapped up the parcel; then she brought Mrs Anderson's basket and wheeled it to the door for her, forcing a passage through the crowd with skilled determination while Mrs Anderson, not a great deal taller than she was, followed.

What a nice child, Mrs Anderson thought, walking on. She stopped at the newsagent's; no daily paper had arrived that day, and there were none in the shop now, so she bought the local one, and the *Radio Times* and *TV Times* so that she should know what would be available on radio and television for the days ahead. She often bought the *Radio Times* when she was in Framingham, since even when the paper came, its description of programmes was sparse. Plodding up Hatch Hill, she thought the distance grew longer and the hill steeper every time she climbed it. I'm getting spoiled, she thought, riding in cars.

After lunch she had a doze, and then she opened the paper. There was a photograph of a girl on the front page, under the heading GIRL FOUND DEAD IN FIRE-SCARRED KITCHEN. Mrs Anderson did not recognize her at first, but with no other newspaper to browse over, she read on and learned that her plain, kind friend from the supermarket had been killed.

Detective Chief Inspector Sprockett sat in his office in Allington Central Police Station, a twelve-year-old building made of pale brick, with large plate-glass windows that turned the place into a greenhouse in summer. He and Detective Sergeant Crisp were considering the facts about Marilyn Green's death. The print on the cooking-oil bottle was not that of anyone known to the police, but the brand of shoes leaving the footmark had been identified, and the size. They were looking for a man with small feet who had entered the house the night she died. Shoe shops in the area were being questioned about sales of canvas sneakers, but few were bought in winter months and so far there were no results to follow up. House-to-house inquiries in Framingham had produced no information, nor had Marilyn been to the disco in Allington. The only lead, and it seemed to be to a dead end, came from a bus driver who said he had stopped for a girl wearing a coat similar to Marilyn's on Saturday night. The conductor confirmed this, and said she was alone. She'd got off at Framingham station. She seemed a bit weepy, but he'd paid little attention to her.

"The story of her life, poor kid," said Sprockett. "We seem to be getting nowhere."

"What about the cinema?" suggested Crisp. "Would it be an idea to screen her photograph?"

"If they'll play," said Sprockett.

"She must have been somewhere," Crisp pointed out.

Sprockett pulled the telephone nearer. He'd need divisional consent for this. Detective Chief Superintendent Winslow was none too pleased at the lack of results so far, but if Marilyn Green's assailant had not closed the kitchen door upon her body, thus cutting down the draught, his efforts to obliterate the signs of his presence by fire would have been more successful. He just might have got away with it.

CHAPTER
ELEVEN

Kevin went straight home, after he came off the early shift, every day that week. When Jessie got back from the office she found a tea tray ready, and the kettle just boiled. There was always a cake of some kind, a rock cake one day, once an éclair. Kevin himself was invisible but audible, up in his bedroom which he was painting, with the radio tuned to his pop programme.

Jessie decided that this was his way of apologizing for what he had done — locking her out and burning her underclothing. On Thursday, when a doughnut awaited her, she went up and knocked on his door.

After a moment he opened it. She saw that two walls were painted orange and he was putting red paint on the third. The ceiling was yellow. Jessie blinked at its gaudiness. The room had been green and blue before.

"You're busy," she said, trying to put some enthusiasm into her voice.

"You don't like it," said Kevin.

"It's not what I'd choose," said Jessie bravely. "But then, I'm old-fashioned. It's cheerful, anyway. Why don't you come down and have some tea, Kevin? Share my doughnut? It was nice of you to buy it, and those other goodies all the week. You'll have me getting fat."

"I don't want any tea," said Kevin gruffly, then added, "I've had some. Thanks."

"All right, then." Jessie hesitated, then said, "Why don't we go to the cinema, just you and I, like we used to? Wouldn't that be nice? Is anything good on?"

A warm glow filled Kevin at her words. Then she spoiled it.

"Bob's out at a dinner tonight. Men only," she said.

So she'd made her suggestion just because her precious Bob wasn't available. Kevin was about to make a harsh retort but then his mood changed again. Maybe he could still make her like him best.

"There's a war film at the Odeon, Screen Two," he said. A few years ago, Allington's large cinema had been divided into three small ones.

"Right. Let's go, then," said Jessie. "We'll have something to eat and then we'll be off. It'll be like old times."

An hour later they caught the bus at the end of the road for the short ride to the cinema. As a learner-driver, Kevin could not take a passenger on the bike, much to Jessie's relief. She had not noticed that he had taken off the L plates.

Jessie paid for their seats while Kevin bought some toffees, which he knew she liked. They were in time for the advertisements and the trailers heralding future delights. In the intermission before the main film began, Kevin bought some popcorn for himself. He sat chewing it while the fighter pilots of World War Two took to their Spitfires. Halfway through the film, the screen went blank and then the face of a girl, grey on a dark background, was shown. A calm voice spoke.

"This is a police message," it said. "Do you know this girl? She was found dead last Saturday night in Framingham. Her name was Marilyn Green and she was seventeen. The police want to talk to anyone who saw her that evening, or any other time, particularly a young man she may have been meeting. If you think you can help at all, please let the police know. Marilyn Green wore a distinctive coat patterned in orange and green." The picture changed, and a girl was shown wearing the coat. Kevin felt his flesh crawl. "If you saw Marilyn Green, or know anything about her movements, please get in touch with the CID at Allington Central or your nearest police station," the message continued. The telephone number of Allington Central Police Station followed, and the film resumed.

Kevin's impulse was to flee from the cinema, but he forced himself to chew on at his popcorn, if only to drown the pounding of his heart. He took some time to calm down and reflect that the fuzz must be really in a twist to put out something like that. He'd only to keep his cool and it would all die down. What baffled him was why the fire hadn't been more successful. He'd had no trouble before, but he'd had paraffin then. Luckily, the night he took Marilyn to the cinema, he'd kept his helmet and scarf on till he was sitting in the dark. He felt naked tonight, helmetless, although he'd got the new blue scarf. He wrapped it well round his mouth and chin when he and Jessie left the cinema.

Home again, Jessie made tea and they sat in the kitchen drinking it, discussing the film. Kevin liked the

103

dogfights between Messerschmitts and Spitfires and the bursts of flame when one caught fire and spiralled to the ground or exploded, but Jessie preferred the romantic part, the tale of the squadron leader and the WAAF plotter. Kevin seemed in no hurry to go up to bed, and his mood was easier than it had been for weeks, so that Jessie decided she would never get a better moment to talk to him. She took a deep breath and began.

"Kevin, I'm going to marry Bob," she said. It was no good talking in an indirect way to Kevin; he needed to be given the message, straight. "Not for a bit — but in a few months. I'll be moving to his house, and you'll have to find a room somewhere. I'll be letting this house. We'll still see a lot of each other — you'll come at weekends and in the evening sometimes." Her voice trailed away as a blank expression came over Kevin's face.

He sprang to his feet and banged his cup into the saucer so that the tea splashed over the table. His thin body quivered as he loomed over her, his face with its youthful acne close to hers.

"Now you tell me, when I've painted my room — spent a bomb on the paint," he yelled at her, snatching at the first argument he could throw at her to hide his real anguish.

"I'll repay you," said Jessie weakly. "And I told you, it won't be just yet. You'll have plenty of time to find somewhere to live. It'd save you time and petrol if you moved to Framingham."

"Yeah — I might at that. I've got friends there — got a real big place, they have," said Kevin, with bravado, and then suddenly he crumpled. ''You don't want me'' he wailed, like a little boy, and slumped down at the table with his head on his arms, sobbing. ''No one wants me.''

Jessie was trembling.

''Of course I want you,'' she said. ''But you're not a child now. You must stand on your own feet.'' She put a hand on his shoulder, but Kevin flung it off and got up, rushing up the stairs. She heard his door bang.

There were tears in her own eyes as she cleared away the tea things and washed them up.

When she came downstairs the next morning, he'd already got his own breakfast, and gone.

That night, Kevin moved into The Gables. He'd packed a few things in a rucksack before Jessie was up — two clean shirts, socks, a spare singlet and pants, and taken thirty pounds which Jessie kept for emergencies in the drawer of the sideboard. He took a few tins from the larder, too. He'd only got one more day's work before the Christmas break, when Blewett's was closing until after Boxing Day. Jessie would be really scared when she found he'd gone. She'd said something about Bob spending Christmas Day with them and sharing their Christmas dinner; well, they could have it on their own now; it was all one to him. He certainly wouldn't starve at the big house with what the old girl had stashed away there, and an old crone like that would be no problem to deal with.

After work he rode three miles up the by-pass to a transport café where he had fish and chips and several cups of strong, sweet tea; then he came back and turned up Hatch Hill to The Gables.

The light was still on downstairs. It was too cold to hide in the bushes until the old woman went to bed, but there was no need to wait; she'd never hear him entering the house. Kevin wheeled the motor-bike over to the outbuildings and tried various doors. One shed door opened; inside were spades, forks, several mowers, and a wheelbarrow. Kevin wheeled his bike inside and covered it with some old sacks; no one was going gardening in this weather. Then, carrying his rucksack, he climbed into the house through the window he always used.

Standing in the passage, he could hear the sound from the television set in Mrs Anderson's sitting-room. The urge to open the door and confront her, to frighten her, was almost irresistible, but Kevin overcame it: that was a treat to come. He set off upstairs to his eyrie, drew the curtains across the window and turned on the electric fire. He was lying on the bed, listening to his transistor, when Mrs Anderson came upstairs at nine o'clock.

Later, when her bedroom light was out, he went down and helped himself to some blankets. They were stored in a vast cupboard, which seemed to him like a small room, on the landing; there were dozens of sheets, pillow cases and towels, enough for an army, Kevin thought. He took sheets and pillow cases too; he might as well be comfortable and he liked things nice. To round it all off, he cut himself a thick slice from a white loaf that was in the bin in the larder and spread it with jam and butter, eating it as he walked upstairs.

He slept dreamlessly that night and, without his alarm clock or his aunt to wake him, did not stir until after nine o'clock. It was light by then and he was already late for work, so there seemed no point in getting up; besides the old girl might see him if he went out. He rolled over in his narrow bed and soon fell asleep again, the electric fire burning away and Mrs Anderson downstairs quite unaware.

"It's the funeral today," Mrs Clarke told Mrs Anderson. "They'd to wait until after the inquest, you see, and they wanted to fit it in before Christmas. A terrible thing."

Mrs Clarke, who came on Fridays to make gestures with duster and vacuum cleaner around the house, was acquainted with Marilyn Green's family, though only just, for she disapproved of them thoroughly. But she was enjoying her close association with the mysterious affair of the girl's death. She put the kettle on for the cup of coffee which was essential, soon after arrival, to get her through the rest of her onerous two hours' labour.

"She was a kind girl," said Mrs Anderson.

"Knew her, did you, then?" asked Mrs Clarke, biting back the "dear" she tended to tack on, automatically, at the end of any remark. Mrs Anderson did not encourage such friendly ways and was prone to leave the room while her handmaiden enjoyed her coffee, unlike Mrs Clarke's other two employers who liked a chat.

"At the supermarket," said Mrs Anderson austerely. "She was a nice girl." She felt sad: she'd have liked to send flowers to the funeral if she had realized when it was.

"Can't have been too nice, if you ask me," said Mrs Clarke. "Must have asked for it, is what I say."

"It was an accident, wasn't it?" said Mrs Anderson, stooping to gossip because she was concerned.

"Well — hardly, with all the police questions going on," said Mrs Clarke. "Some fellow went into the house after her and did her." Mrs Clarke didn't know if Marilyn had been sexually assaulted; it made a better tale if that was implicit.

"Oh dear!" Mrs Anderson was so shocked at this that she had to sit down. "Oh, Mrs Clarke, what a terrible thing." The paper had merely said that Marilyn's body had been found in the kitchen where a fire had burned itself out. She had been wearing her outdoor coat, and was severely bruised. There had been no mention of foul play. "Murder?" Mrs Anderson asked.

"I suppose that's what it comes to," said Mrs Clarke.

"Poor girl," said Mrs Anderson. "How dreadful!"

"Hanging's too good for them," said Mrs Clarke with gusto. "Them as does such things."

Mrs Anderson was inclined to agree.

Pleased with the effect of her opinions, Mrs Clarke rose to mop the kitchen floor.

"I shan't be seeing you until the New Year," she said. "That's in a fortnight. My Bert has a holiday next week."

"Oh — I hadn't realized," said Mrs Anderson. Mrs Clarke's desultory efforts irritated her so much that she often thought of sacking her, but she would never find anyone else to come out so far, and if she were ever to be ill or have an accident, Mrs Clarke eventually would arrive and find her.

"Most firms shut till New Year," explained Mrs Clarke.

"Very well. I wish you a happy Christmas, Mrs Clarke," said Mrs Anderson, and she handed her her wages, and an envelope containing her Christmas cheque. Mrs Clarke in turn surrendered a tiny parcel in holly paper which on past form would contain a piece of soap.

"Good of you to spare the time to come today, when you must be so busy," said Mrs Anderson, but her sarcasm was wasted.

"I couldn't let you down, I couldn't live with myself if I did," said Mrs Clarke, winning that bout.

Joe Knox was due in the afternoon, with the paraffin, and after that Mrs Anderson could expect to see no human face until Muriel Dean came to collect her on Christmas Day. That was not unusual; she seldom saw anyone after Mrs Clarke and Joe on a Friday until her next shopping trip on Tuesday. Next Tuesday the shops would be shut, and it would be Thursday before another shopping expedition was due. Even the refuse men would not be calling to collect the garbage; Mrs Anderson's large dustbins, filled from her smaller bin kept beneath the sink and emptied on Wednesdays, would not be dealt with again for at least ten days. Suddenly her solitude pressed down unbearably on Mrs Anderson; the silence in the big house seemed an almost tactile thing, full of soundless noises. She switched on the radio to break it, and heard the laughter of a panel game.

Joe came at three o'clock with the paraffin. He left an extra supply because he wouldn't be coming for a fortnight either; by cutting Mrs Anderson off his long round, he need not disappoint his other customers and could make up the lost days of the holiday.

Mrs Anderson gave him his bottle of whisky. When he had gone, she was alone, and by four o'clock it was dark.

CHAPTER
TWELVE

A barrel-organ played carols in the street on the last shopping day before Christmas, while its attendants shook collecting boxes at the passers-by. Muriel Dean saw that the object of their charity was the Third World and evaded their importunings, for in her opinion much charity was still required at home. She was on her way to buy Brussels sprouts. Everything else was in the larder — a large turkey, a fresh one — no plastic-wrapped, frozen, flat-breasted bird for her — mince pies made, and the cake iced. Howard had brought the car up to the High Street to fetch the drink; he should have gone to the off-licence earlier, Muriel thought, seeing the crowds and the double-parked cars. She put the sprouts in the car and then, to fill in time, because Howard would be ages, she went along to Pandora's. She'd bought some Elizabeth Arden bath powder and a box of chocolates for Mrs Anderson — old people were unlikely to buy luxuries for themselves — but there might be some other small object here which would appeal; she was determined to give the old lady a happy day. If only there were a letter from Australia in reply to hers to cap it, but it was too soon for that.

She found Emily packing up a mother bear and her

cub, both dressed in green checked gingham, for a large, spectacled man.

"You are busy," said Muriel. "Trade must be good."

"It's been like this all month," said Emily, handing over the parcel. "I've scarcely thought about Christmas myself yet."

"Are you going to June's?" June was Emily's married daughter who lived in Wales.

"No — too far — I mightn't get back if it snows," said Emily, taking the money from the next customer who had selected a fibreglass tray with an elaborate design of fishes.

"Why don't you join us on Christmas Day?" said Muriel. "Share our turkey? We've got a large one and we're eating it at lunch time. There'll only be Howard and me, and old Mrs Anderson from that big house on Hatch Hill. I don't suppose you know her."

"It's kind of you, Muriel, and I'd like it, but I've already got Janet and Laura coming to me."

"Bring them along too, then," said Muriel. "It will be nice to have a child around, and it will do you good to have a rest. I won't hear of a refusal."

Emily made no attempt to give her one.

"It would be lovely," she said. "Thank you."

Now Muriel would need more gifts. She couldn't very well give Emily and Janet something from their own shop, so she decided to make toiletry her theme this year and went to the chemist's, where she bought bath oil for Emily and toilet water for Janet. The newsagent's had a small toy department, and there wasn't much choice left among its wares, however Muriel found a card game there played in crossword shape rather like Scrabble, and hoped that would be suitable for Laura.

Driving home with Howard, she told him where she had been.

"They're all coming to lunch on Christmas Day," she said. "Emily, Janet, and the little girl."

Howard was too stunned at the news to reply.

Kevin grew restless as Saturday wore on. He wanted a proper meal, and he hadn't had a bath since he moved in. He lay on the bed in the attic room brooding about how he'd been turned out of his rightful home by a fat old man with a loaded wallet. He was the one to blame for Kevin's plight; before he came along, everything was all right. He needed teaching a lesson.

At intervals, Kevin went on to the landing and down the first flight of stairs to see if the old woman had gone to bed, and at last she came up. He heard the radio from her room.

Kevin slipped downstairs without waiting for her to switch off the light; she wouldn't hear him with the radio on. As he passed the telephone, which stood on a table in the icy hall, just to be on the safe side he cut the wires with his sharp, stiletto-like knife.

The old girl had been shopping. There was fresh butter in the refrigerator, and two vacuum-sealed packs of bacon as well as some fresh-cut rashers in a plastic box. There were sausages, two small chops, a chicken, and there were plenty of eggs. Kevin took butter from a dish on the larder shelf and fried himself two eggs and two pieces of bread, some bacon, and three of the sausages.

They burst, oozing pinkly, because he cooked them too fast. He followed them up with a banana; there were four in a bowl. He didn't wash up. Then he went out to the shed and unlocked it. He wheeled his motor-bike along the drive and into the road, then free-wheeled down Hatch Hill, kicking the engine into life only as he turned towards the by-pass. He rode straight to Allington, slowing down as he drew near his aunt's house.

Bob Watson's car was outside.

That did it. They should have been out looking for him, not carrying on with their disgusting behaviour as though he didn't exist. Cursing aloud, Kevin swung the bike round and accelerated away, roaring through the town until he reached the southern outskirts where Nairn Road was. He'd followed Bob home more than once and knew just which was his house, and now it was empty.

The houses in Nairn Road all stood in a quarter of an acre of ground, with trees and shrubs screening them from each other. There was no one to see Kevin park his bike just inside the gate of 35 Nairn Road and slip round the back of the house. He tried all the doors, and the windows, but everything was securely locked and so was the garage.

"Suspicious bloody bugger," Kevin muttered to himself.

Shielding his torch with his hand, he explored the garden. There might be a ladder somewhere. He found a shed, tucked close the boundary hedge, the door fastened with a bolt and padlocked. Kevin soon hammered the latch free, using a heavy stone, and inside, just waiting for him, was a large can of paraffin.

Laughing to himself, Kevin went back to the house with the can. He thrust his gloved hand through a glass pane in the door of a sunroom built on at the rear of the house, and unlocked it. The door from the sunroom to the room beyond was also glass-paned; he broke that glass too and unlocked the second door. Then he splashed paraffin over Bob's hallway, the sitting-room carpet, the chairs and the sofa. The fire was laid in the grate but not lit. He'd start it from there. He went up the stairs with his can, but it ran out halfway so he had no paraffin for the upper floor.

He went back to the sitting-room and held a lighted match to the paper in the grate; it burnt up and the dry sticks, neatly placed, began to crackle at once. Kevin took one out and, holding it carefully, went with it into the hall, where he dropped it into the pool of paraffin soaking into the carpet. Then, as it flared, he let himself out of the front door, banging it behind him.

Straddling his bike a little way up the road, away from the street light, he waited. He wanted to be sure of this one. It wasn't long before he saw a glow behind the drawn curtains at the front of the house. Exultant, he stayed until the curtains themselves were flaming, and then he rode off, before someone else saw the fire and raised the alarm.

Emily and Janet totted up their takings on Saturday night and when they saw the size of their total, Emily poured them each a sherry from the bottle kept in the back room.

"Our shelves are almost bare," said Janet. "How do we have a January sale?"

"We don't. We won't buy in any seconds," said Emily. "We're known for our quality. Now, you go and collect Laura and I'll lock up and dump the cash."

"Will you be all right?" said Janet. "Wouldn't you like me to go with you?" It was usually Janet who put the takings in the bank's night safe.

"Of course I will. Muggings don't happen in Framingham," said Emily.

"You can't be so sure. Remember that poor girl last weekend? That was in Framingham, and it sounds like murder."

"No one is going to mug white-haired old me on my way to the bank," said Emily.

"Well, take care," said Janet. "See you on Christmas Day."

"Ah — Christmas Day — I knew there was something I had to tell you," said Emily. "Plans are changed. Muriel Dean has asked us all — you and Laura as well as me — to go there. They're having some old lady Muriel's being kind to to lunch, and they want us too."

"Oh!"

"It's difficult to say no to Muriel," said Emily. "And I didn't try — she'll do us proud."

It would save Emily so much trouble; there was no way to avoid it, Janet saw. She scarcely knew Muriel; they had met in the shop a few times, and that was all.

"It will give great offence if we don't go," said Emily firmly, seeing the doubtful expression on Janet's face. "And it might do a good turn to Howard, who'll otherwise be stuck with just our Mu and the old dear, whoever she is. Muriel's a great one for lame dogs."

116

"It's very kind of her," said Janet. Visiting Howard and Muriel at home would be a strange experience, and one she was not eager for, but there was no help for it.

He rang up that evening.

"I hear you're coming on Christmas Day," he said. "It's marvellous." But he sounded none too positive.

"Is it?" said Janet.

"Yes. I'd been hoping to see you over the holiday," said Howard bravely. He had been with her, as usual on a Friday, the previous evening and had not mentioned this aspiration then.

"Is Muriel out now?"

"Yes. She's just gone to deliver a parcel to one of her protégés."

Of course he wouldn't risk telephoning if Muriel were in the house.

"All right. See you on Christmas Day, then," said Janet, ringing off before there was the slightest risk of Howard being caught in the act of telephoning his mistress by his kind, unsuspecting wife.

The boy and girl, both wearing jeans, the boy in a padded anorak and the girl wearing a thick, grey duffle coat, sat on upright chairs facing Detective Chief Inspector Sprockett in the cinema manager's office at the end of the Saturday night programme. During the film, after the police message and the display of Marilyn's photograph, they'd discussed in a whisper what to do, the boy not wanting to get involved but the girl insistent, and now they were carrying out their resolution. The manager had, with reluctance, because

117

he would be late home, telephoned the police for them.

"We did see her — not last week, it wasn't, but the week before," said the girl. "I noticed her coat. They came into the cinema ahead of us and sat near us, in the back row." She blushed a little. She was a pretty girl, thin and fair, and very young.

"That's right," said the boy, committed now. "She was with this fellow in motor-cycle gear — helmet and that. I didn't see his face. Wasn't interested."

"Did you get a good look at him?" Sprockett asked the girl.

"Not really. I was looking at the film, you see. It was really frightening." She'd clutched at Ray in terror, and he'd been only too ready to comfort her.

"Well, was he tall or short?" asked Sprockett. "Did you notice that?"

"Oh, he was a little fellow," said the boy, who was almost six foot tall himself. "It was just his helmet that made him seem tall. He'd got it on, you see, even going into the cinema. White, it was, and he'd a scarf round his face. That was white too, sort of."

"What about when the lights went up in the cinema? In the intermission? There was one, wasn't there?"

The manager confirmed that there was, but the two had noticed no more about their neighbours; they were absorbed with one another.

"The girl had a helmet too," said the boy. "She wasn't wearing hers. It was orange."

It was a start. They could begin checking motorcyclists to find out where they were on the crucial night. Sprockett sighed at the task and wondered how many men he must ask to forgo their Christmas leave.

"We'll need to talk to your staff," he told the manager. "The usherettes. The girl in the ticket booth. The ice-cream girl. Whoever runs the kiosk."

"They've gone home," said the manager.

"You've got their addresses, haven't you?"

"Yes."

"Make a list, please," said Sprockett. He turned to the young couple. "I'll have to ask you to come to the station to make a statement," he told them.

"We'll miss the bus home," said the boy.

The girl had paled.

"My mum'll kill me," she said.

"We'll get a message to your parents," said Sprockett, nodding at Detective Sergeant Crisp who had been making notes as they talked. "And we'll send you both home in a car."

That'd be a real help, thought the boy. But there was nothing else for it.

After Bob had gone, Jessie went upstairs. She stood in Kevin's room. Three walls and the ceiling were freshly painted; the fourth and the door were not yet done. His razor and flannel were still in the bathroom, but she had missed some tins from her store, and with a sinking heart she'd looked in the drawer where she kept her emergency fund of ready cash to find it had gone. She'd told Bob that Kevin seemed to have left home, but did not mention the money. Maybe he'd come back when that was spent; he was just trying to frighten her. It was one thing to tell him he must find somewhere else to live before long; quite another for him to go off in a rage.

She looked in his drawers. He'd taken some under-clothes and shirts. Kevin was a great one for clean clothes and he wouldn't go away without reserves; she wondered if he'd found someone — some girl, perhaps — who would do his washing.

Under his sweaters, in the bottom drawer of his chest of drawers, she found the white scarf he usually wore. She drew it out and looked at it. One end was singed, blackened and frayed at the fringe. Wondering anxiously how he had burned it, she did not realize that the brown smears on the scarf were bloodstains. She put it back, remembering that he had worn a blue one when they went to the cinema.

Bob hadn't wanted to leave her that night, but she'd insisted. Kevin might return.

Kevin grinned as he sped through the night on the bike. He wondered if Bob's house would burn right out before the fire brigade was called. There didn't seem much going on in the road when he left, so it might not be noticed for some time. The longer the better: that would show the old man who was tops. Kevin would have liked to start the fire while Bob was there, but that would have meant problems: Bob was no dozy old lady and his house was not a huge great place like The Gables; he might hear an intruder, and he was a large man. Besides, there hadn't been time for much planning.

He put his motor-bike back in the shed at The Gables and covered it over. Then he relieved himself against the side of the shed before going into the house. He was halfway up the stairs when he remembered the washing-up and he went back and saw to it: no point in spoiling things just yet. He'd see how the next days went. It wouldn't take much to make the old girl die of fright and no one would ever know the truth of it. Then he'd be able to live here at his ease, for surely no one would ever miss her.

Before going upstairs again, Kevin took a tin-opener from the kitchen drawer, a cup and a plate and a knife, to make meals in his room more civilized. He fancied a bath; but if he ran one now the old girl might hear him. He knew she used the small bathroom near her room but there was another, larger one at the front of the house; why shouldn't he use that while she was running her own bath? She wouldn't hear him above the noise she was making herself. He'd try it tomorrow.

When Jessie would not let him stay with her, Bob had tried to persuade her to go back with him to Nairn Road, but she would not agree.

"Never mind if you are out when Kevin gets back," Bob had said. "Do him good." He did not add that her zealous concern for the boy might be cramping his style with girls; he was probably with one now.

"He went off because I'd told him our plans," Jessie persisted. "We'd had a nice evening at the cinema and then I spoiled it."

"Well, he had to know sometime," Bob had said.

In bad moments he wondered if he and Jessie would ever succeed in marrying, for the problem of Kevin seemed too difficult for her to resolve. During the years he had seen Jessie about the offices he had known nothing of her private life, and only discovered that she had made a home for her nephew when she was lent to his department during the illness of his assistant. One night they had worked late to clear up some details for a meeting the next day, and he had driven her home. It had started then, with a gentle, undemanding friendship which Bob gradually realized offered him the prospect of ending his loneliness. He wouldn't give it up easily.

"He's doing it to punish me," Jessie said. Bob didn't know about her burnt underwear in the bath. "He wasn't at work today. I rang up. I didn't ask if he was there — just asked to speak to him. Mr Blewett said he hadn't turned up."

"Hmph! Taking time off for Christmas," said Bob.

"He might have had an accident, riding off in a temper," said Jessie. But he probably wasn't in a temper when he left; he'd have cooled down into that icy calm, which in a way was more frightening.

"The police would soon let you know if he'd had an accident," said Bob.

"I suppose he'd have something on him to show who he was," said Jessie doubtfully.

"His driving licence would, and there's always the registration number of his bike," said Bob. He'd tried to ease her gently out of her anxiety but he hadn't been very successful. He'd even suggested going away for a few days over the Christmas holiday, to a hotel, and forgetting it all, but Jessie wouldn't agree.

Bob turned into Nairn Road and drove towards his

house. As he drew nearer, he saw ahead of him the blue, blinking light of a police car and, beyond, two fire engines. A cluster of people stood on the pavement watching the activity. Bob parked his car at the side of the road and got out. Lumberingly, in his heavy overcoat, he ran towards the scene for he could see already that it was his house upon which the hoses were turned.

Jessie did not learn about the fire until the next day, when Bob telephoned her early. He had spent the night with the neighbours who had seen the blaze in the lower part of his house and had raised the alarm. It was a clear case of arson: that had been established as soon as the firemen were able to enter the building, for they found an empty tin, scorched and dented, in the hall, and Bob confirmed that a tin of paraffin had gone from the shed. The broken lock on the shed door was a further proof.

He told Jessie all this on the telephone. The ground-floor rooms of the house had been badly damaged; broken glass in the doors at the back showed how the firebug had entered.

''The police haven't any idea yet about it,'' Bob said. ''It may be some crazy monster who just picked on me by chance. Or it could be someone who imagines they've some sort of grudge against me.''

Icy with shock, Jessie knew just who that person was, and thought it could not be long before Bob realized it, too.

CHAPTER
THIRTEEN

Mrs Anderson looked at the small, mangled lump of butter in the dish in the larder. She'd put out a new piece cut neatly off the block only the day before, and could remember eating a little with a slice of bread and some cheese at supper time. Most nights in the winter she had instant soup from a packet, with bread and cheese; in summer she ate lettuce and tomatoes instead of the soup. She'd bought four bananas on Thursday and only three were in the bowl. There was only half a loaf left in the bread bin, too, and it had been jaggedly cut. She always cut the loaf neatly, and one lasted her for several days, often going stale before it was finished. She'd bought two for the weekend, and two packets of bread mix in case she couldn't get out again when the shops re-opened.

Trembling, she sat at the kitchen table, her breakfast forgotten, trying to recollect her actions the evening before. She saw herself pouring the hot water on to the soup and stirring to mix it well. Was it tomato soup, or chicken? Or possibly oxtail? She couldn't remember. So perhaps she couldn't remember sawing at the loaf, hacking it, and eating a banana? She got up and looked in the garbage bin and sure enough there was a banana skin in it, and two egg shells. She'd had no eggs: or had she, instead of cheese? She couldn't remember at all. Like a dog scuffling for a bone, she burrowed under the egg shells and found her instant soup packet: it was chicken. She sat down again, breathing deeply, trying to steady the uneven beating of her heart, unable to remember anything about the banana and the eggs, and after a few minutes she got up and went to the larder, checking her tins against the list. They balanced. She stared at the wall where the paint had begun to peel. How could she have eaten all that bread, and the eggs, and forgotten?

Mrs Anderson went into the sitting-room and with shaking fingers lit the paraffin stove. She sat down in front of it, her thin arms crossed over her scrawny chest, rocking herself back and forth in her distress. She tried to recall what she had done last night. She'd wanted to be in bed for the radio play; she always went to bed in time for that on Saturdays. She'd had the soup — she remembered the chicken flavour now — a piece of bread and some cheddar cheese, a wedge from the new piece she'd bought at Fresh Foods. But it seemed that she must also have scrambled or poached the eggs and consumed them on hunks of bread. Perhaps she had come down in the night and had a midnight meal, half asleep, but surely then she'd have had indigestion? Indeed, she did feel a little sick now. How extraordinary to come downstairs in the night and eat, and then forget all about it, but she'd heard that sleepwalkers never remembered their night excursions. There had been those other times, the empty bean and spaghetti tins, the coffee cake, too few bananas left, the money she couldn't remember spending.

Mrs Anderson sat there alone, not crying because she never wept now, but moaning to herself. How could she go to the Deans' the next day in this state? She might have another attack of forgetfulness and behave eccentrically. After a while she went out to the hall to telephone and say that she could not come, first finding the number in the directory — *Dean, H. J., Beech Ho., Grove Rd.*, that must be it. But when she lifted the receiver, to dial, the line was dead. Mrs Anderson jiggled the rest but nothing happened. She seldom used the telephone these days but she liked to feel it was there and she made enough calls to know that it sometimes behaved erratically. She would try it again. If it was really out of order she would have to go to the nearest telephone box, which was in Framingham, to report it.

She went into the kitchen and saw her breakfast all set out, untouched. She'd forgotten about it.

Her wits really must be going.

Mrs Anderson put the radio on for the church service but she scarcely heard it, her mind squirrelling round in panic, wondering what would happen if she really became incapable of managing her own affairs. Perhaps she should write to her solicitor in London, warning him that she was failing, preparing him for the need to protect her. But old Mr Sykes had retired and there was a new young partner who would he impatient and who wouldn't understand about Billy. That was an added problem of age; everyone else was so young.

She decided to open a tin of rice pudding for lunch, for although she didn't feel much like eating, she must have something. She fetched the tin of rice pudding from the larder, altering the list to tally, but she couldn't find the proper opener in the drawer. There was a spare one, not a very good one, and she cut her hand using it so that she had to go to the cloakroom cupboard for a band-aid to stop the bleeding. She warmed the rice pudding in a pan on the Aga and forced herself to eat it, though really if she'd had all that in the night, she shouldn't need food today.

Mrs Anderson tried the telephone again in the afternoon but it was still quite dead. Outside, it was sleeting, and she could not possibly go out to report it in such weather. Perhaps it would be working again in the morning. Exhausted by her fears, Mrs Anderson fell asleep in her chair and felt calmer after her rest. She picked up her knitting and turned on the radio. There was the *Messiah* to listen to, and other Christmas programmes. If I concentrate hard, she told herself, I'll overcome this little bout of forgetfulness; it's just that the winter is rather depressing.

She tried the telephone again before going to bed, but without result. When Muriel Dean arrived in the morning she would have to explain that she wasn't well enough to go out, and why she had not been able to telephone to say so, and ask her to report the faulty line to the engineers.

Jessie had screwed herself up to tell Bob what must have happened. He came over on Sunday morning after spending hours with the police and fire brigade. Neighbours had helped move a lot of the furniture to the garage, but everything was soaked by the firemen's hoses. Jessie had put the piece of pork she had bought for herself and Kevin in the oven, and had prepared vegetables, for Bob must eat even though she wouldn't be able to swallow a morsel. She poured him some sherry from the bottle she kept for him, and with her face turned away from him, asked if the police knew who had set the fire.

"No." Bob sipped his sherry. He'd really have liked a beer but Jessie had this idea that sherry was suitable. She'd soon learn his ways.

She turned to face him.

"It was Kevin," she said.

"Oh Jessie, now think what you're saying! That's a very serious accusation to make," said Bob.

"He'd a reason," Jessie insisted.

"He may not like me, and he may not want to leave this nice home you've had together, but that's a far cry from setting fire to my house," said Bob.

"Don't tell me you didn't suspect him," Jessie said. "No one else could possibly have anything against you."

"Well, the thought did cross my mind, I admit," said Bob. "But I dismissed it."

"Did you mention it to the police?"

"No!" He was outraged.

"Kevin's done it before," said Jessie. "He started the fire that killed his mother."

"Oh no!" Bob stared at her. "You can't know that," he said.

"I'm sure," said Jessie. "But it could never be proved. There was no trouble about it at the time."

"He was only a child."

"He was eleven — nearly twelve. His mother had a — a friend, Leonard Davis, living with her. Kevin was jealous so he started the fire and his mother died. I don't suppose he meant to hurt anyone," said Jessie baldly.

"But that's dreadful!" said Bob.

"The police thought it was an accident — the paraffin stove, you see, which Kevin had lighted in the night. Then he'd gone back to bed. But Len knew. And Kevin, of course. And I did, though I didn't let myself think about it. We never talked about it." She thought of her burnt underclothes. "He has lit other small fires now and then, when he's been upset, but only little ones," said Jessie. "There was never any real damage."

If she was right, thought Bob, the boy must be out of his mind.

"What are you going to do?" he asked.

"Tell the police," said Jessie. "He can't be allowed to go on. Someone else may get hurt." She remembered the scarf in his drawer, and its burn marks; how had that happened? "There's a meal ready," she said. "There's no point in wasting it. Let's eat first and then perhaps you'd take me to the police station, Bob."

In some undefined way, Jessie thought that a delay, however small, might help Kevin.

"Why do you think your nephew would do such a thing?" the detective constable asked.

"He — he likes fire," Jessie said.

She did not want to betray Kevin totally, but in the end she had to reveal her suspicions about the fire that killed Kevin's mother; she did not say she was certain, now, of his guilt, and she did not mention her own burnt underclothes.

Waiting for her, Bob thought her brave. It all added up — the surliness, the way they had been locked out of the house, and then the terrible tale from the past. The boy needed a good leathering, Bob decided in one mood, and in the next felt pity for the youth who was so mixed up and insecure. He was grateful for the qualities of his own son, now thirty and married with a son and daughter of his own. There was a lot in luck. A boy needed a man about the place when he was growing up, and Kevin's father seemed to have been absent for ever; but that didn't mean he was bound to become delinquent. Bob had known men killed in the war whose widows had brought up their sons to be good citizens, but a dead father who was a war hero was a different kettle of fish from a petty criminal who resorted to violence. Jessie had told him the sorry tale. She'd wanted to see the police on her own, and Bob understood that, sitting in the car; when they caught Kevin — and they would, Bob was confident — it would be very hard for her, although the boy need not know it was she who told them about him.

She came out of the police station at last, and they went straight round to Bob's house, where they spent the rest of the afternoon salvaging what they could of his possessions. Nothing could be done about the insurance until after the Christmas holiday.

Seeing Bob's car, the neighbours who had put him up the previous night asked them both in for drinks. It was, after all, Christmas Eve. So when Detective Sergeant Crisp and a detective constable called at Jessie's house, wanting to look through Kevin's things to see if there were any clues as to where he might have gone, they found no one at home.

It could wait. The identity of the probable arsonist was known, and the registration number of his motor-bike. He'd very likely turn up quite soon, spotted by some road patrol, and a few hours' delay going through his belongings wouldn't make much difference. Crisp went home, and sent the constable off too. Christmas or not, they'd call on the aunt the next day.

Kevin slept late on Sunday morning. It was half-past nine when he looked at his watch. He swung himself out of bed, in pants and singlet, and pulled on his jeans. The room was warm, heated by the electric fire he had left on all night, but on the landing outside it was very cold. He pattered down the stairs and paused, then went along to the old lady's bedroom and listened outside the door. There was no sound. He turned the handle and looked in. The room was empty, the bed made, bedroom slippers neatly placed beneath a chair, kettle, cup and saucer on a tray. He went out again, closing the door, and walked along the landing to the front bathroom where he relieved his bursting bladder. The water in the pan was rusty and there was a strong smell of disinfectant; now and then, Mrs Clarke poured a bucket of water into it, and some bleach. Kevin did not try to pull the chain — it was an old-fashioned, lofty cistern — but he turned one of the taps on the bath. Nothing happened.

He left the bathroom and went down the main staircase into the icy hall. He could hear nothing, but she must be in one of those rooms, the kitchen or that sitting-room with all the photographs.

Kevin went back to the old woman's bedroom and looked at the tray on which she kept her tea things. There were tea bags in a tin. He filled the kettle in her bathroom and put it on, staying in her bedroom till it boiled, and made himself tea in her china pot, which he took upstairs to his attic. He ate a tin of salmon taken from Jessie's larder, opening it with Mrs Anderson's tin opener. He didn't like the tea milkless, without sugar, but it was warming. He'd fix things better in future, he thought, returning the rinsed teapot to the old woman's bedroom; he didn't want to confront her till he was ready.

He spent much of the day drowsing, with his transistor on, and when he was awake he remembered the fire he had set and the rich glow of it behind the curtains in Bob's living-room. That'd teach him. He had no sense of guilt, and he had almost forgotten Marilyn.

He ate cold baked beans from a tin later, but by the time Mrs Anderson came up to bed he was longing for something hot. He didn't wait for her to put out her light, but slipped downstairs and fried himself three more of the old girl's sausages, some bacon, eggs and a thick slice of bread. He made himself tea, ladling sugar into the cup and stirring it with the same spoon, and he ate another banana. He cleared up quite well after himself, for he was often neat in his ways.

CHAPTER
FOURTEEN

The sleet turned to snow during the night, and on Christmas morning there was a powdering everywhere, enough to look picturesquely seasonal but cause no problems to travellers. Mrs Anderson woke with the feeling that the day was somehow different, and took a little time to remember her invitation. She'd intended to say she couldn't go to the Deans', she now recalled, but she felt suddenly alert, spry, almost restless. It would be ungracious to refuse to go after Mrs Dean had gone to the trouble of coming to fetch her. Mrs Anderson looked out of the window at the white, wintry world and wondered if the snow would prevent her from getting the car out, but she saw that blades of grass, twigs and stones pierced the white covering, and there was only a film on the dark branches of the trees.

She got out of bed and walked stiffly into the bathroom. Her morning bath eased her joints. Once, she had slipped getting out of the water and she was very careful now, holding on to the rim of the bath and then sitting on a chair, afraid of falling. She did not want to lie on the bathroom floor with a broken hip slowly perishing from exposure.

She ran the bath, washed her thin body with the blue

flannel, and lay for a few minutes letting the hot water soothe her stiff joints, her white hair pinned up in a skimpy plait. She should have washed it in honour of the invitation, but if she did, she would be quite exhausted when Mrs Dean arrived. Mrs Anderson had given up going to the hairdresser when the once-quiet salon in Framingham abolished its individual cubicles and installed basins all down one wall. Some things should be done in private, so Mrs Anderson let her hair grow and cut it herself when it straggled on to her shoulders. *Pensioners half price,* she read in the window, passing the hairdresser's, but Mrs Anderson did not like these concessions to age; she had always paid her way in full and meant to continue that way.

She would put on her best dress today, a mauve wool button-through style in soft wool that she'd bought by post several years ago. When she needed new clothes now, she bought most of them in response to advertisements, but she had once had a well-stocked wardrobe and she still wore garments she had had for years. Under her wool dress today she put on clean underclothes, a vest and bloomer knickers. She fastened her stockings to her corset belt; when it wore out, it could be hard to find a replacement for such things might no longer be made. She'd lost weight since it was new, but she was used to its stiff support, and she resisted the efforts of salesgirls in the draper's in Framingham to persuade her into tights.

It might be cold at the Deans', so she took her old fur stole downstairs. She often wore it in the winter. Long ago, the central heating had worked well, operated from

135

the boiler in the cellar, but to run that now would cost a fortune. Mrs Anderson had had the radiators drained off so that there was nothing to be damaged by severe frost. The front bathroom was out of action too.

She took the porridge pan from the Aga's low oven. In winter, every night before going to bed, she put oatmeal and water in to cook slowly; in the morning it was ready, piping hot and soothing. There was nothing to throw away when she finished, so she didn't see the egg shells that Kevin had disposed of into the garbage bin the night before, but the loaf was jagged again, and much smaller than she recalled. She neatened it with a corrective slice, frowning. Feeling brisk, as she did today, it seemed incredible that she should be doing these strange things; perhaps she'd been having a bad few days. She must just pay more attention to what she was doing, that was all.

Marilyn Green's mother was busy in the kitchen of the Rose and Crown on Christmas Day. She'd got Fred a little job today, helping clear dirty glasses from the bar and mop tables; he'd get his dinner for that, and a few pounds, not to mention tips from generous customers. He'd been a bit quiet lately, since their spot of trouble.

Ena peeled potatoes and prepared sprouts with a thoroughness absent from similar labours performed in her own small, dark house. Today, over a week after Marilyn's death, her mother had still not really taken in what had happened. The police had spent hours examining every inch of the house minutely and going through all Marilyn's possessions. They'd asked her and

Fred over and over again to try to remember if the girl had mentioned meeting someone the night she died, but she never told them anything. Marilyn contributed to the rent and the cost of what food was prepared at home: she cleaned the kitchen most Sundays. Otherwise she spent much of her time in her own room reading magazines or listening to the radio, or knitting herself jumpers from patterns in those magazines. Now a source of income had been abruptly cut off and a maid-of-all-work had been lost. Occasionally Ena felt there was more to it; she hadn't liked it when the constable sorted through Marilyn's things with his large, red hands, but she did not recognize grief, or guilt.

''It's good of you to come today, Ena,'' said Mrs Crow, who ran the Rose and Crown with her husband and did all the cooking. ''But it helps to take your mind off it, doesn't it? No good sitting at home and brooding, eh?''

''That's right,'' agreed Ena, gathering up sprout outer leaves into a sheet of newspaper.

''How are the police getting on? Have they made any progress?'' Mrs Crow didn't want to spend long on the subject, she was too busy, but it would be heartless not to show sympathy, and besides, she was curious. Last year Marilyn had come in on Christmas Day as an extra waitress. She'd worn a dark dress and white apron, and despite her size and plain looks had been a success, pleasant to the customers and, though slow, efficient. She'd come in several times since to help out when there were dinners. It seemed dreadful that she'd been somehow knocked about and killed, though no one really knew just what had happened, it appeared. Ena had said there'd been a fire, and that someone had been in the house with Marilyn. Who'd knock her about unless they were after something she wouldn't let them have? But there'd been no sign of that, it was rumoured.

"I don't think they're getting anywhere," said Ena. The police had put their fingerprint powder all over the place. "I don't think there was anyone there." Marilyn was always clumsy; she'd caused her own death, tumbling over and pulling the pan after her. She'd never have brought a fellow into the house — she never had, anyway. Unless she'd been carrying on secretly. It didn't seem likely.

Howard and Muriel looked at the snow that had fallen while they had slept, and over breakfast discussed whether to ring up their daughters then, or later. It might be too early for them, they decided; they'd call in the evening. Then they opened the presents they had bought for each other — a pullover for Howard and a bottle of port, and a leather handbag for Muriel, just like her old one which was wearing out, with a cheque inside.

"Thank you, darling," said Muriel, kissing Howard.

He held her for a moment, feeling the familiarity of her sturdy body, the faint scent of lavender water which was all she ever used, the strong strands of her greying hair against his cheek. Once he had loved her with passion; he respected her qualities and still held her in affection. He did not want to leave his comfortable home but his heart was full of that thin young creature with her curly dark hair and her exciting, slender body; she made him feel as if, before he met her, he had been only half alive. He longed for her when they were apart, yet paradoxically, he was always glad to get home to his own surroundings. In imagination, he sometimes transported Janet and Laura to Beech House, with Muriel miraculously vanished, though not dead — perhaps, improbably, swept off by another. There was space in this house — a study for him if Janet's lampshade-making and patchwork filled the sitting-room, as it did in her own house, and the big garden for Laura. Under this new regime, he would be restored to youthfulness himself, Framingham society would accept the change and he would retain the respect of his old friends.

Janet was coming today. Howard prayed that they wouldn't give themselves away, or that Laura, in her innocence, would not do it for them.

"That's a nice little girl of Janet Finch's," he said. "I've met her when I've been getting Janet to sign things." Saying this would, he hoped, forestall any surprise Muriel might feel when Laura greeted him with recognition. "Your old lady," he went on. "Shall I fetch her for you?"

"Oh no, thank you, Howard," said Muriel. "She'll be expecting me. The snow isn't much — it'll be all right. I'll get everything organized before I go and the pudding will be quite safe for that little time. The pan has to be kept topped up with boiling water," she explained, as if Howard had not been familiar with these preparations for over twenty years.

"I'll lay the table," said Howard. He'd open the claret to let it breathe, and he'd be one up on everyone by having a drink before the guests arrived. He was going to need it.

Bob and Jessie spent the night before Christmas together, tenderly and without passion, in the double bed she had inherited from her parents. She had cried a good deal and he had done his best to comfort her, but at the same time reflecting grimly that once young Kevin had been found he would be locked up for some time and in no position to cause her more distress. When he came out of prison he might have learned some sense. Meanwhile, Bob knew that the problems connected with getting his house made habitable would not be easily solved and the work would take months. The simplest thing would be to persuade Jessie to marry him soon; then he could move in here while the repairs were made without tongues wagging. It did not occur to the law-abiding Bob that the police might find the case against Kevin hard to prove, even if they were sure he had set the fire.

Jessie's sobs diminished, and were replaced by the even breathing of slumber. As she rolled on her side, away from him, he tucked himself against her, shaping his body to hers so that they were like two spoons, wishing briefly that she was in fact his dead wife, with whom he had so often lain thus comfortably linked; then he fell into a steady, deep sleep himself.

The police arrived soon after breakfast, their footsteps ruffling the layer of snow that had fallen in the night. It

140

was Detective Sergeant Crisp, whom Jessie had met at Allington Central Police Station, and a detective constable she had not seen before. They apologized for their early, unseasonable call and explained why they had come.

Jessie agreed that they could certainly go into Kevin's room and examine his belongings, but she didn't think they'd find much to help them.

"You haven't found him?" she asked, forlornly.

"Not yet. He may be a long way off by now," Crisp said. "He could travel, on the bike. But if he's still using it, we'll soon pick him up."

He would use it: he loved that bike, if he loved anything, and he would not know that the police were looking for him. He'd never suspect her of betraying him. What excuses could be found for him, to get him the lightest possible sentence, Jessie wondered, leading the men upstairs.

"He'd been repainting his room," she explained, opening the door.

The policemen did not even blink at the vivid hues. Crisp's expression remained stolid as he observed the cans of paint standing on some paper in a corner, with a well-cleaned brush on the top of one of them. There was a strong smell of spirit in the room.

"I don't know why he didn't put all that out in the shed," said Jessie.

"Boys have their ways," said Crisp obscurely. "We won't keep you, Miss Swales, if you've things to do. We'll call if we want any help."

"Yes — well — " Dismissed, Jessie still hovered. "I

expect you'd like some coffee. I'll make it, for when you've finished."

She pattered downstairs. Bob was taking her out to lunch at the Bell Hotel in Allington, the main hotel in the town square. All the tables had been reserved well in advance, but Bob knew the manager and had been able to arrange it.

"I don't know what they think they'll find," Jessie said. "Kevin never got any letters. There'd be no address or anything." But there'd been that girl, the one he said he was meeting that Saturday, and he'd mentioned friends in Framingham.

"They have to look," said Bob. For all he knew, there were wax images of himself, stuck with pins. The boy must have hated his guts. It was a horrible feeling, knowing that someone wished him so much harm.

Jessie refilled the percolator. It had been strange, waking up with Bob. In the night she'd woken and heard him snoring softly. It hadn't upset her; she'd kissed his nose and he'd grunted a little, moved in the bed, and then the snoring had stopped. She'd never spent a whole night with a man before, though there had been her heartbreaking romance when she was young with Tom Cash, who was married. He'd worked in an insurance office. They'd talked of running away, of Tom leaving his wife and two children. Their affair had gone on for years, and now she thought Tom had probably never had any intention of leaving his wife. But then there had been the fire when her sister died, and after that there was no more talk of running away and no more snatched sessions on her bed. Since then, there'd been nothing. Of course, Bob wasn't young; he wouldn't be like Tom. But then, she wasn't a girl any longer. It would be all right.

The coffee was perking well when the detective constable tapped on the door and asked her if she could spare a minute.

Jessie hurried upstairs, smoothing her palms on her grey jersey skirt for they felt suddenly clammy.

In Kevin's room the drawers from the chest had been stacked on the bed. Crisp had found the white scarf. He held it up, balanced on the end of a ballpoint pen. She could not think why he did not hold it properly.

"Can you identify this as your nephew's scarf?" he asked.

"Yes. He always wore it — until just recently, that is," said Jessie. "He'd got a new one, a blue one." She'd already told them that, when they'd asked her how he was likely to be dressed.

"He didn't mention why he'd changed?"

"No. I didn't ask."

"When did you notice he was wearing the blue one?" Crisp asked. "Can you remember how long he'd had it?"

Jessie remembered that he'd worn the blue one when they went to the cinema together.

"I didn't see him going off to work," she said. "And not always when he got back." Then she thought of the evening she'd been expecting Bob round and was cooking, when Kevin had come into the kitchen and stuck his fingers into the bowl of cream. He'd been wearing the white scarf then; he'd pulled it away from his face and it had hung loose round his neck. "He was wearing the white one — this one — the Saturday before last," she said. "And the blue one when we went to the cinema on Thursday. Why?"

The policemen looked at one another.

"Do you know how this one got scorched?" Crisp asked.

"No. Perhaps he caught it on the stove," said Jessie. "Lighting the gas to put the kettle on?"

"Perhaps he did," agreed Crisp. He didn't draw her attention to the rusty brown stains that could be blood.

Detective Constable Mitchell opened the wardrobe, revealing the orange helmet on the shelf where Jessie had put it. Beside it was a Marks and Spencer's parcel, and below, some shirts and a denim jacket hung on wire hangers. Crisp already had the feel of this house, the neat fastidiousness of Jessie Swales, bordering on the genteel, and the inadequate boy afraid to break away and yet not able to conform.

"This is a new helmet," said Mitchell.

"Kevin's was white," said Jessie. They knew that already.

"Have you seen this one before?" asked Crisp.

"Yes." Jessie told him where she had found it and that she had put it away. Mitchell was taking it out of the cupboard, holding it gingerly by the end of the strap. He dropped it into a large polythene bag.

"Any girl friends, your nephew?" Crisp asked.

"I — he said he was taking one to the cinema," Jessie said. What had this to do with Bob's fire?

"When was that, Miss Swales?"

"Oh — two weeks ago — just over," said Jessie.

"To tell you the truth, I wasn't sure if he was making it up," she added.

"Why?" asked Crisp again.

Jessie explained, blushing a little, about Bob coming round that evening.

"When did you find the orange helmet?"

"The next weekend," said Jessie. "A week ago last Saturday."

Crisp glanced at Mitchell.

"Did he know a girl called Marilyn Green?" he asked.

It was Mitchell who had made the connection, Mitchell who had seen in his mind's eye the photograph that had been flashed on the cinema screens and who had read the report of the couple seen at the cinema, the youth in a white crash helmet and with a white scarf across his face, the girl carrying an orange helmet.

"I don't know," said Jessie. "Who's Marilyn Green?"

"She's dead, Miss Swales," said Mitchell. "I'm sure you must have read about it in the papers. She lived in Framingham. Only seventeen. Beaten up and died. There'd been a fire in the kitchen where her body was found."

Crisp frowned at him. There was no need to go on.

But Jessie remembered now, and she remembered the two beer glasses she'd found in the house the night she put the orange helmet away. She'd washed them up, and taken the empty bottles out to the shed. She looked at Crisp and literally felt her scalp prickle.

"We'll be taking these things away, Miss Swales," Crisp said. "I take it you have no objection. The

145

constable will give you a receipt.''

Jessie nodded slowly.

''Have you found anything to — to give you some idea where he's gone?'' she asked.

''No letters. Just a few magazines,'' said Crisp. ''No diaries or notebooks.'' Sometimes there were, in such cases. Poor bitch, she'd had a body blow. It had taken some guts to shop the little bastard, but all she thought he'd done was start a fire, and now she'd something much worse to face. She hadn't missed the point; she wasn't slow. There would be plenty of prints here, even if she'd polished round since the boy left, and there was the cooking oil bottle with its solitary specimen: enough to convict Kevin Timms if it matched.

Crisp left Mitchell at the house until Forensic could get there. The scarf might yield a lot of information: the blood group, for instance, from those stains; traces of lipstick if they'd been necking. With it wrapped in a polythene bag, Crisp drove off feeling quite cheerful. This would make a nice Christmas present for the chief inspector.

CHAPTER
FIFTEEN

The lights on the Christmas tree in the bay window of Beech House shone out as Emily turned her yellow VW beetle in at the gate. The snow had been swept from the drive, the garage door was open, and the car was gone. So Howard was out, no doubt fetching the other guest, Janet thought, as Emily parked.

But it was Howard who opened the front door and came to greet them. He kissed Laura first, then Emily, and finally Janet, very chastely on the cheek.

They trooped in and took off their coats, which Howard bore off to the cloakroom. Then he led them into the sitting-room where a log fire burned in the grate, holly decked the pictures, and Christmas cards hung on strings across the room. The lights of the tree, a tall one with a tinselly fairy on the top of it, made a splash of brilliance, and the whole atmosphere was warm and welcoming.

Janet glanced round curiously. There was a large, comfortable sofa in front of the fire, with armchairs on either side of it, all covered in a deep rose-coloured linen with a floral design; the carpet was plain green and so were the curtains; and the walls were a very pale shade of green, almost white. The effect was restful.

There was a large poinsettia in a pot on a low mahogany chest, and some old prints on the walls.

Laura saw parcels on the tree. She clutched one herself, wrapped in dark green paper with a fir tree motif and tied with gold string, Stilton cheese in a pottery jar for Howard and Muriel. Janet and Emily had both left bottle-shaped parcels on the hall chest. Howard was urging them to sit down; he pushed one of the big armchairs nearer to the fire and seemed to think Emily should sit there, then settled Janet in another. He poured sherry for them and Coca-Cola for Laura, who had perched herself on the sofa, swinging her legs.

Laura liked Howard. She saw him frequently, although she was usually on her way to bed by the time he arrived, except on Fridays, when he came straight from the station with his briefcase and umbrella. She accepted his visits without curiosity; they were just part of her life. He often brought her presents — sometimes a book, sometimes sweets, once a puzzle.

"Muriel is fetching Mrs Anderson," Howard said. "Do you know her, Emily? She lives in that isolated house on Hatch Hill, and Muriel has adopted her."

"I've never met her, but I may know her by sight," said Emily. "Isn't she a bit of a recluse?"

"Of necessity, I imagine, stuck up there," said Howard.

Listening to them, Janet felt very strange, sitting in Muriel's chair in Muriel's room where she had lived for so long with Howard. She wondered what he was thinking. He seemed a little uneasy.

"Ah — here they are," he said now, and there was

unmistakable relief in his voice at the sound of a car outside. He hurried from the room and went to open the front door. Voices came from the hall, Muriel and Howard's, and a faint murmur from the old lady.

In the car, Muriel had explained who the other guests were. Mrs Anderson, already anxious, felt nervous at the prospect of meeting still more people, but she remembered the nice little girl who had looked after her at Pandora's, and her pretty, curly-haired mother. Having got so far, she would not be daunted by sheer numbers. When she entered the room, Janet and Laura both recognized her, and stood up, coming forward to greet her with friendly smiles. Mrs Anderson could not know how grateful Janet was for the diversion she made.

A high, wing armchair was pulled up to the fire and Mrs Anderson was put to sit there, and given a sherry. She looked tiny and frail in the big chair, her fur cape round her shoulders, her lined face pixie-like. Muriel set a small table close to her, for her glass. Everyone smiled kindly at the old lady. She took a sip of sherry, feeling slightly disoriented; the comfortable room was rather like the drawing-room at The Gables years ago and she half expected the boys to appear. The strange feeling soon passed and Mrs Anderson began to feel glad she had come, but it was so long since she had been part of a social occasion that she found it hard to think of any small talk.

Laura, however, was waiting for a chance to speak. She got up from the sofa and gave Muriel the parcel she held.

"This is for you," she said. "Happy Christmas."

"How lovely," said Muriel, taking the package. She looked at it, smiling, then held it up and shook it very gently. "I wonder what it can be? I'll put it under the tree for now and open it when we've had lunch." She crossed to the tree and set the parcel down beneath it, stooping so that her jersey dress pulled tight round her buttocks.

"Oh, get mine, Laura, will you, dear?" said Emily, and Janet gave her a nod too.

Laura made two expeditions to bring the other parcels in from the hall and when she had laid them carefully with the rest, Mrs Anderson beckoned her over. She extracted her modest offering, wrapped in festive paper, from her handbag and gave it to Laura to put with the others.

'How exciting," said Muriel. "Now I'm going to see if the turkey is ready. Laura, will you help me?"

Laura followed Muriel eagerly out of the room, and Janet listened while Howard began to talk to Mrs Anderson. As he leaned intently towards her, Janet could see the familiar balding patch on his head. She looked away and said brightly to Emily, "Laura will love helping but I wonder if there's anything we can do?"

"No, relax. Muriel will have everything under control. She's a masterly organizer," said Emily, who admired Muriel because she did not fritter away her considerable energy but channelled it usefully. Emily had noticed the expression on Janet's face when Muriel and Laura left the room together, and the look she cast across at Howard, and a suspicion that Emily had had for some

150

time was strengthened. Well, it was really not her business, but Howard was an idiot; in the end someone would get hurt, and it would probably be all three of them. Janet was young, pretty and lonely; Howard was bored with familiar, plump and middle-aged Muriel; but he'd never give up his established home and position for love in a cottage with Janet. He was just having a final fling. Emily hoped earnestly that Muriel suspected nothing. If she did, she wouldn't have invited Janet today, unless she was cleverer than Emily thought her.

Emily leaned across to Mrs Anderson.

"Have you known Muriel long?" she asked.

Mrs Anderson explained how they had met, and while they were discussing the problems of getting into Framingham from Hatch Hill, Laura came in, wearing a checked apron much too big for her over her best outfit, the brown pinafore and bottle-green sweater.

"Lunch is ready," she said. "Please go into the dining-room," and she ran out again, calling to Muriel, "I told them."

Howard moved to help Mrs Anderson out of her chair but she got up quite alertly, and stepped forward, pulling her stole round her, looking up at him with a little smile which illuminated her wrinkled face. He led her into the dining-room and settled them all in the places Muriel had ordained earlier, with Mrs Anderson on his right and Emily on his left. Laura was to sit on Muriel's left next to Mrs Anderson, and Janet on her right, beside Emily. While they were arranging themselves, a small excited face appeared at the hatch between kitchen and dining-room and Laura asked, "Are you ready?" She turned then, and announced to Muriel, "They're sitting down nicely, except Howard."

A few moments later a procession came into the dining-room, Muriel carrying the turkey on its large dish, and Laura a silver tray with the gravy and bread sauce in silver sauce boats. The vegetables were already on the table in green and white china dishes.

The meal was merry, largely because of the mood set by Muriel with Laura. The little girl enjoyed the importance of helping her to serve it, and could be heard uttering encouragement as Muriel set the brandy alight over the pudding. The food was perfectly cooked and perfectly served, but without any fuss, so that everyone, even Janet, felt comfortably relaxed. She had had two glasses of sherry before lunch, and now Howard's claret took away her anxieties for the present; the future could wait.

"If it snows some more, I won't be able to go to London tomorrow, will I?" Laura asked, finishing her pudding, in which she had found a shiny new ten pence piece.

"Er — well — it depends," said Janet. She explained to the others, "Laura's father is taking her to see *Peter Pan*."

"I want to see *Peter Pan* but I don't like going in Daddy's car," said Laura. "It makes me sick."

"I took my boys to see *Peter Pan*," said Mrs Anderson. "Years ago, it was. Long before the war." They'd clapped and clapped to save Tinker Bell.

"Where are your boys now?" asked Laura.

"Two are dead. One is in Australia," said Mrs

Anderson.

"Oh, that's very sad," said Laura. "I'll come and visit you, if you like. It's a good deed to visit someone old."

"Laura!" Janet cried in horrified reproof.

"I'd like to come," Laura went on, regardless. "I could do little jobs for you."

"That's kind of you, my dear," said Mrs Anderson, amused. "And I should like to see you, but I live at the top of Hatch Hill and it might be too far for you."

"It wouldn't be," said Laura. "I've been tobogganing on Hatch Hill."

"Well, we'll see," said Janet, still mortified.

Howard and Mrs Anderson went into the sitting-room while the others cleared away and loaded the dishwasher.

"This is so kind of you and your wife," Mrs Anderson said, resuming her throne-like seat in the high armchair. It was years since she had eaten turkey. Alone at The Gables, Christmas was just another day to be got through.

"I'm delighted that you could come," said Howard. "This is a time when the house should be full."

It was six o'clock when Mrs Anderson was finally taken home. After all the parcels had been opened, Muriel found a box of Spillikins sticks and Mrs Anderson had several contests with Laura; then she taught the little girl some of the paper games she had played with her sons, like Battleships. They had watched part of the circus on television, and though Mrs Anderson did not care to see performing animals, she enjoyed Laura's pleasure; there were some good jugglers. Tea had appeared, with a fine iced cake adorned with a small Father Christmas and his reindeer that Muriel said she had used for years.

Muriel was so nice. She was dull, dowdy, plump; but she was so thoroughly nice, Janet thought, and knew, with sad resignation, that the bonds of time and habit that linked her with Howard were too secure to be seriously threatened by an outsider.

Howard took Mrs Anderson home through the fine snow that had begun to fall.

"I can never repay your kindness," said Mrs Anderson, on her doorstep, with the bath powder that Muriel had given her in a carrier bag together with a large slice of the Christmas cake, a package of cold turkey and six mince pies.

"Just let Muriel come and see you sometimes," Howard said gently. "It will stop her worrying about you, out here on your own. She does care, you know, and she needs people who will let her."

Mrs Anderson nodded, understanding him.

When he had gone, she realized that she had forgotten to mention that her telephone was out of order.

Muriel, tidying up, thought it comic of that nice little girl to address Howard by his first name while politely calling her, throughout the afternoon, Mrs Dean.

CHAPTER
SIXTEEN

Kevin heard the car that came for Mrs Anderson at half-past twelve on Christmas morning. He'd lain awake a lot in the night, after sleeping so much the day before and after his heavy meal, so that when he did drop off, once again he slept on till after nine. Carols on the radio reminded him what day it was. In his cupboard at home was a parcel containing a nightdress which he'd bought for Jessie at Marks and Spencer's in Allington; he'd spent twenty minutes wandering among racks of nylon and printed cotton before making the important choice of a white nylon one with lace trimming round the bodice. Well, she wouldn't be getting that now, and it was as well since she'd have been sure to wear it for that old man.

Kevin lay on his bed feeling sorry for himself for some time. Then the demands of his bladder proved too strong, and as on the day before, he went down to the front bathroom. He spent longer there today, and replaced the lid afterwards. There was some paper, funny stuff in a packet.

He went downstairs and listened outside the sitting-room door while Mrs Anderson sat inside with the radio on. A man intoned and then a carol began. Kevin knew it, *Once in Royal David's City*, he'd sung it at school. He imagined opening the door, bursting in and giving the old dame a surprise, and he got as far as turning the doorhandle, but in the end he decided to wait and went upstairs again, shuddering at the cold in the passages. He refilled Mrs Anderson's kettle in her room and made tea, but again there wasn't any milk. Back in his room he opened a tin of Jessie's pilchards which were horrible on their own, and he chased them down with some tinned pears: a curious breakfast.

He was looking out of the window at the snow-covered garden when the car arrived. He saw it circle round outside the house, leaving tracks in the snow, and then it disappeared from his view.

Kevin went to the top of the stairs and listened; he heard the front door close, then silence. In seconds he was at the first-floor landing window, watching the car depart. The old girl had gone out for her Christmas dinner and he had the place to himself! He felt like shouting in his relief but there was something inhibiting about the house that stopped him. He'd make the most of the opportunity, though: and the first thing was a bath.

In Mrs Anderson's old cast-iron bath, whose enamel was iron-stained under the taps, Kevin lay in ten inches of water, soaping his skinny body with Mrs Anderson's Lux soap and washing his lanky hair. He'd taken a towel from the cupboard where he'd found the sheets; it was huge, nearly as big as a blanket, though a bit thin in places. When he'd used it to dry himself, he mopped up the bathroom with it, soaking up the splashes he'd made on the lino-covered floor. He shoved it, a damp bundle, back in the linen cupboard afterwards. There was Vim and a cloth in a corner, and he cleaned the bath. Then he went up to his room and put on fresh underclothes and a clean shirt. He washed the others in the kitchen sink, squeezed them hard, and took them upstairs in a bowl so that they did not leave a trail of drips. He hung them round his room to dry.

Now it was time for his Christmas dinner. He went into Mrs Anderson's larder to see what he could find. There were two sausages left and a rather small chop. Among the tins were plenty of vegetables, and some tinned ham. He selected a tin of ham, one of carrots and another of peas, and heated the vegetables in their tins by standing them on the Aga hotplate. He fried the ham, cut into chunks, in a pan. Mrs Anderson's better tin-opener was now up in his room but he found another one which served. He peeled, very thickly, two large potatoes from some in a bag in the larder, and fried them too, in butter. They were hard, half-cooked though brown outside, but he ate them, wiping the plate and the pan with a slice of bread. Then he ate a banana. That left only one. He rinsed his plate under the tap and put it away, and wiped out the pan, replacing it on the shelf at the side of the stove. Then he went into Mrs Anderson's sitting-room and lit her paraffin heater. He prowled round, looking at the photographs lined up on every shelf and ledge, the male faces at varying ages. He came to her desk and opened the lid. Inside was a pad of thin writing paper and some airmail envelopes. There was a fountain pen and a bottle of ink. In a drawer were some assorted stamps. There were a few receipted bills in a pigeon hole. Nothing interesting.

He opened the top drawer and found more writing paper and envelopes and a packet of headed postcards, from which he learned his involuntary hostess's name and that of the house. The second drawer contained several dozen letters in airmail envelopes just like the unused ones above. Kevin picked one out. It was addressed to William Anderson, Esq., at an address in Queensland, Australia. That address had been scribbled out and *Gone Away. Return to Sender*, written beside it. Mrs Anderson's address was scrawled in black ink in the space left. Kevin turned the envelope over and saw the same name and address, Mrs Anderson, The Gables, Framingham, Herts, England, neatly printed on the flap. He lifted the letter out and read, *My dearest Billy,* and then an account of the writer's doings. The letter was dated four years previously. Kevin looked at more of the letters. They were all the same, all addressed to William Anderson at the Queensland address and all marked *Not Known*, or *Gone Away*. The bottom drawer of the desk contained photograph albums and a cardboard file full of receipts.

Kevin could not make out the business of the letters. He did not try for long, but switched on the television set and watched for a couple of hours with a tumbler of sherry poured from the bottle of Harvey's which he'd noticed in the cupboard. It was quite an effort, after that, to return to his attic room, but the old woman might be back soon.

She must be loaded, living in a house this size, with all

these rooms, although, to Kevin's eye, most of the furniture looked like junk. He'd get some money from her, frighten her into giving it to him, then he'd scarper — get right away. He'd set himself up with the loot. Later, when he was doing all right, he might send for Jessie to join him — by then she'd be properly fed up with Bob.

He didn't work out what his enterprise would be; he just dreamed of success.

Divisional headquarters had sent out a telex to all stations to be on the look-out for Kevin Timms, wanted for questioning in connection with the death of Marilyn Green as well as the fire in Nairn Road.

Detective Chief Inspector Sprockett studied the reports in his office on Christmas Day, while outside the citizens of Allington enjoyed their holiday. Prints found in Kevin's bedroom matched the one on the cooking-oil bottle, but it was too soon for a pronouncement about the bloodstains. A long brown hair had been found in the orange crash helmet, and that, if Marilyn's, could be identified. There was plenty to talk about, when the youth was found. Very likely he was miles away by now, in someone else's patch, but he was not a practised villain like his father, with contacts who might help him; he was a loner, friendless and unpredictable. He'd attacked the girl mercilessly, and set the fire in Nairn Road from spite or malice. He might commit another violent act and harm someone else if he was not found soon. It was routine that brought results; routine, following information received, had revealed the connection between Kevin Timms and the dead girl to observant, experienced police officers, and routine procedures would ensure his ultimate conviction.

Sprockett's wife had switched their Christmas dinner to the evening, and his two daughters aged six and eight were quite excited at the idea of staying up for a candlelit meal, wearing their party dresses. He went home at last, unable to do more to apprehend Kevin Timms.

Mrs Anderson walked through the cold hall of her house to the cloakroom and hung up her camel coat. She took off her hat and put it on a peg. Various coats, jackets, caps and scarves hung there, including an old tweed cap of Billy's and a raincoat. A pair of his boots stood among hers on the floor. Mrs Clarke often suggested sending them to a sale, or putting them away upstairs, at least, but Mrs Anderson liked to see them there, reminding her that Billy might be back at any time. It occurred to her that she had not seen the blue woollen scarf Helen Combe had given her one Christmas, and which she sometimes wore, for a while. She hunted among the garments on the rail, but there was no sign of it. Could Mrs Clarke have taken it? Much as Mrs Anderson deplored Mrs Clarke's general lack of enthusiasm for her job, she had never thought her dishonest, though it was true that she arrived late and left early, and that was dishonesty of a sort. She'd mention it, next Friday. But then she remembered that Mrs Clarke wouldn't be coming until the week after.

She went into the sitting-room, expecting to find it

bitterly cold, as it always was if she was out and the fire not lit. But the room felt quite warm. Mrs Anderson lit the heater which had had time to cool down since Kevin turned it out. Then she went into the kitchen with the bag of good things that Muriel had given her. She put the mince pies and the cake in tins in the larder, and the turkey in the refrigerator. She had eaten so well that she did not need any supper; she'd have a cup of Ovaltine and perhaps a mince pie later on.

Mrs Anderson sat in her chair by the fire, her fur stole round her shoulders, thinking over the day. It was the happiest, Christmas or otherwise, that she had spent for a very long time. Everyone had made her feel welcome. Closing her eyes, she thought back over the years to when her boys had been small and had brought their laden stockings into her bedroom on Christmas morning to display their contents. There were the big presents later, downstairs by the tree. One year Harry had been given his bicycle, a shiny black one with three-speed gears. Jack had been a train enthusiast, gradually acquiring the Hornby electric set that was now upstairs. Billy had liked his fort with the lead soldiers; she'd kept them all. She thought about the toys, still upstairs in the attic. She turned off the heater and went out of the room, pulling the fur stole close against the cold.

Mrs Anderson slowly climbed the stairs to the first floor, shivering in the bitter draught that blew along the passage. The wind was rising, and it was snowing hard now. She put her hand on the banister rail of the upper stairs. She had not been up here for months, but now, on Christmas night, she wanted to go to the big cupboard in the attic room and look at the toys her sons had played with so long ago. She began to ascend.

She heard the faint sound of the radio as she reached the top landing, and she saw the light under the door of one of the rooms. Mrs Anderson had a sense of total unreality as she put her hand on the door knob and turned it. The warmth from the room came to meet her as she opened the door. Her incredulous gaze took in the youth on the bed, in jeans and singlet, a magazine in his hand and the radio playing pop.

CHAPTER
SEVENTEEN

It was hard to say who was the more shocked, Kevin or the old lady. He sat up, staring at her as she stood in the doorway, one hand to her skinny chest as her strong old heart began to flutter, and she gave a little choking cough as she caught her breath. Kevin did not hear the sound above the noise his radio was making. He swung his thin legs in their tight jeans off the bed and with three quick strides was standing over Mrs Anderson, hands raised as if to strike her. She winced, screwing up her eyes to focus on the pale face so close to hers; he had a fuzz of soft, light hair on his chin and upper lip. Mrs Anderson took a step backwards, then made herself stand firm as training instilled in her Edwardian childhood reminded her that she must not show fear. Kevin's reaction when she moved was just as instinctive: with the flat of his hand he slapped her face, so that her head was knocked to the side and she banged it against the door post. The pain was sharp and tears filled her eyes. She blinked them away, hand to the bruised spot, feeling herself sway, but now Kevin gripped her arm. Pinching it tight, he twisted it behind her back and held her, glowering down at her. A faint, sour smell came from him: the smell of fear.

"You — you — " he sought for words to hurl at her and uttered the obscenities he knew.

The tide of words washed over Mrs Anderson as she fought the pain in her arm and the weakness that threatened to overcome her. She tried to breathe deeply and evenly to make her heart stop bumping about and give her the appearance of calm. Finally Kevin paused for breath.

"Release me at once," said Mrs Anderson, but he held her more tightly. An agonizing pain shot up her arm. She stood firm.

Kevin did not like the feel of her skinny arm in its wool sleeve against his fingers. He didn't like touching anyone, not now. Once, long ago, there had been softness and warmth that made him feel safe; never since. He'd never wanted Jessie to kiss him when he came to live with her and he'd pushed her away when she tried. He sought no tenderness anywhere, for it would be false. The only contact he understood was when he was dominant — with the machinery of his motor-bike, when he struck Marilyn, and now, with the old lady at his mercy. The bones of her arm were stick-like under their covering of almost fleshless skin; he could easily snap them between finger and thumb, but they repelled him and he let her go.

"Don't try any tricks," he said.

Mrs Anderson resisted the urge to rub her aching arm. She let it hang by her side, pressing it against her body. The giddiness caused by the blow to her head was passing and she was turning questions over in her mind. Who was this youth? How had he got in? She knew she had locked up properly when she left the house that morning. He must be some vagrant who had broken in while she was out. There was something vaguely familiar about him; perhaps she had seen him somewhere in Framingham.

"Who are you?" she demanded.

Kevin laughed, a horrible, quite mirthless sound.

"Never you mind," he said. "Get on downstairs and make me something hot to eat." Since he'd been discovered, he might as well reap the benefit.

Mrs Anderson was not sure that she had the strength to obey. She took more deep breaths, and as she did so she noticed the condition of the room. There were sheets and blankets on the bed; there was the electric fire burning; a dirty plate, with a knife resting on it, was on the bedside table. There were magazines piled on the dressing table in a neat stack; a shirt hung on a hanger from the picture rail. She was not able, at once, to deduce what these signs indicated. She turned away and began to walk along the landing towards the top of the stairs; her knees trembled but she hoped the youth would not notice. She could feel him following close behind, and once he put his hand on her shoulder, which was still covered by the fur stole, and gave her a shove.

"Get on with it, grandma," he said.

The one thing she was not, to her knowledge.

Mrs Anderson grasped the banister rail with her right hand and started down the stairs ; she held her left hand against her breast to still the beating of her heart. If he pushed her again she would fall. She held on tight. This young savage should not succeed in doing what life itself had failed to do over such a span of years: break her self-control.

"Downstairs," Kevin said again when she reached the first-floor landing.

She walked on, placing her feet carefully, trying to hold up her head though she felt her whole body shaking; all the time she expected another shove but Kevin contented himself by taunting her. "Get on, get on, you old cow," he said, and more of the same.

Progressing downwards, Mrs Anderson slowly absorbed the evidence of the attic room. The youth had been in the house long enough to find sheets and blankets, the electric fire, the plate and knife. She thought of the egg shells in the garbage bin, the jaggedly cut loaf, the missing tins, and in spite of her predicament a great joy filled her: she was not going senile; he had been in the house for some days, even weeks, and he had taken these things. At the moment she would not admit the shock of violation this knowledge brought; that must wait, and with it the answers to the questions it provoked: where was he from? What had he done in her house? Had he watched her, without her knowledge? Spied?

She walked ahead of the boy towards the kitchen, whose door was closed to keep in the warmth.

"Get in there, cow," Kevin snarled, pushing her again.

Mrs Anderson opened the door and moved in quickly, before he could push her yet again, surprising herself by her own agility. Kevin banged the door behind them and caught her by the arm once more, dragging her over to the larder. ''Not got much in there for Christmas, have you? I suppose you've been out at some swank hotel stuffing your rotten face,'' he said. ''I saw you go out with your swell friends. I watched you. Old bag.''

''Are you afraid of me? Is that why you keep insulting me?'' asked Mrs Anderson. ''Or is it the house that frightens you? Is that why you hold on to me?''

Kevin dropped her arm.

''I'm not afraid of anything,'' he snapped.

''Are you not? Fortunate young man,'' Mrs Anderson said. ''Not even the police?''

''They won't find me. They won't look for me here,'' said Kevin.

''Are they looking for you?'' Mrs Anderson asked, beginning to feel braver. There was a bottle of brandy in the larder, and if he would leave her alone in there, she might be able to swallow some. It would clear her head and pull her round. She couldn't hope to escape from the house unless the youth fell asleep, and even if he did, in the dark and with snow falling heavily, as it was when she last looked out of the window on her way upstairs so short a time ago, she doubted if she had enough strength to get help; it was so far to the nearest house or a telephone box. Now she understood why the telephone was not working: he must have cut the wires.

''What do you know about the police looking for me?'' Kevin asked suspiciously. They weren't; they couldn't be.

''I don't,'' said Mrs Anderson. ''It was your idea. You said they wouldn't look for you here. That means they do want you. What have you done?''

She was twisting his words, and he scowled, lifting his hand to hit her again. Instead, he pulled the fur stole off her shoulders, put it on the floor and trod on it in his canvas sneakers. That wasn't enough for him, and he felt in his jeans pocket for the matches. He picked up the stole, took it to the sink and there, under her appalled gaze, set fire to it. The fur sizzled, emitting a sharp, acrid smell and a lot of smoke which made Kevin cough, so he ran water to put it out. He turned to her, face grim.

"Get in that larder, grandma, and make me some supper," he said. "Or you get it, like that bit of rabbit."

It had been sable. Her husband had given it to her many years ago. She stood looking at him, aware that he was evil, not merely some sort of vandal.

"Go on," Kevin said and pushed her towards the larder. "Get in there, I told you already." He raised his hand to strike her.

"Don't hit me," she said sharply.

Her heart was pounding again. How long could it hold out, racing like this? She pressed both hands against it and looked at him defiantly. She had so little to lose: a few months: a few years at most.

Kevin pushed her aside and went over to the door leading to the hall. He pushed the heavy kitchen table against it.

"You won't shift that in a hurry," he told her, panting with the effort, standing to face her with his hands on his hips, ribby chest rising and falling fast. "Now, I'm not telling you again. Cut the cackle and make me a meal, quick. Something hot."

168

Mrs Anderson went into the larder, trembling. She opened the refrigerator and took out the plate of turkey slices Muriel had given her.

"Get on with it," Kevin growled from behind her. He sat down in the armchair, his back to the barricaded door. "And no funny business. You'll be sorry if you try anything."

In the larder, Mrs Anderson managed to swallow some brandy, straight from the bottle, while delving for potatoes and sprouts. But now she needed to use the sink. She put the vegetables down on the wooden drainer and looked at the charred wreck of her stole. The room was still smoky, and she coughed as she bent to take a pail from the cupboard below, putting the ruined thing in it. She set it to one side, working slowly as she prepared the vegetables, trying to plan, still coughing now and then. Suppose she put aspirins in his meal, lots of them, to make him fall asleep? There was a bottle in the cloakroom.

She tried. She gathered her courage and told him she wanted to go to the lavatory. Sighing deeply, he moved the table and went with her down the hall to the cloakroom but he stood outside the lavatory door and she had no chance to open the cupboard which was in the outer cloakroom. She looked at the high window in the lavatory; a younger person could climb through it and run off to safety, but she could not.

On the way back to the kitchen he made her stop while he went into the little sitting-room. He collected an opened bottle of sherry and a tumbler and brought them back with him into the kitchen, where he sat drinking while she resumed her preparations for his meal. She saw that he was quite familiar with the house and the knowledge was horrifying. He finished the bottle while she prepared the food.

At last it was ready. She'd warmed up four of the mince pies she had been given, and she laid the table with a cloth, as she did for herself every day. Kevin watched as she took it from a drawer in the dresser and placed knife and fork ready at one end of the table, then salt and pepper in shining containers that looked like silver but couldn't be, of course.

Mrs Anderson laid a place for herself too, at the other end of the table. She had no appetite at all, but knew that she must make some attempt to eat; she must keep up her strength for what might be a long night, and she must establish a moral ascendancy over this dreadful youth. Merely to sit there while he ate, waiting upon him, would indicate servility.

Kevin, shovelling the food into his mouth, did not glance at her while she ate a tiny slice of white turkey meat, a fragment of boiled potato, and two sprouts. She managed one mince pie; the pastry was delicious. Her heart had steadied now. She did not think the boy would kill her yet, unless from fear. He belched loudly at the end of the meal and she winced. Kevin noticed, and belched again, rubbing his stomach. Mrs Anderson had always reproved her boys for their belches, if she heard them. She carried the dishes to the sink and washed them up. Kevin watched her silently. She was much slower than Jessie, but she did not fumble.

"How old are you?" he asked at last.

"Very old," said Mrs Anderson, drying the last plate. "Born in the reign of Queen Victoria." She took off her apron and hung it on a peg. "I suppose you've heard of Queen Victoria?"

"What do you think I am? Stupid, or something?" Kevin growled. "Course I have."

"I don't know what you are. You haven't told me," said Mrs Anderson. She stiffened the muscles in her legs, which seemed to be about to give way. She felt dreadfully tired. "Shall we go into the sitting-room?" she suggested, as if to a welcome guest. "It's more comfortable in there."

She went to the door and stood there, waiting for him to open it. Kevin did so, and she sailed ahead of him into the hall, turning on the light. If they left all the lights on, and someone passed and noticed, it might be thought unusual, but who would pass on Christmas night? And anyway, even with all the trees but the firs bare of leaves, the house was scarcely visible from the road.

But Kevin was carefully trained by his aunt and he turned off the kitchen light and the one in the hall behind them.

"Light the fire, please," said Mrs Anderson in the sitting-room, handing Kevin the matches. It was a risky invitation, after what he had done to her fur, but she was not going to stoop down with her back to him, exposed to another blow, as she would be if she were to light it herself.

Kevin took the matches. Once again he thought of tipping the heater over and letting the precious oil run out, the lovely bright blaze leap upwards, but that was a wild idea now, in the night. This was a place he could hide in for a long time, almost for ever, and he must not destroy it: not till he had no further use for it.

Mrs Anderson sat in her own chair. Kevin sat opposite her on the chesterfield after he had lighted the fire.

"Well, what shall we talk about?" asked Mrs Anderson.

"Who said we'd talk?"

"It's customary, after dinner, and especially since this is Christmas Day," said Mrs Anderson. "Well?"

"Well, what?"

"Well, what have you got to say for yourself?"

"Nothing," said Kevin. "I'm not saying anything."

"Very well." Mrs Anderson folded her hands in her lap and waited. He would not sit still for long.

She was right. First he began to fidget, swinging one leg, crossed over the other, up and down. Then he got up and went to look at the photographs, to escape her pale blue stare.

"All them — " he waved his hand at the array of her family. "All them photos — " his voice trailed off inquiringly.

"My husband, and my sons," said Mrs Anderson. "And over there, my parents." She pointed to where the couple sat stiffly, her mother with curled bangs on her forehead, her corseted figure displaying the proud bust and small waist, her father with splendid moustaches, standing beside his wife with a hand resting on the back of her chair.

"Them all your sons? How many?" said Kevin.

172

Mrs Anderson took command.

"Bring me those from the end of the mantelpiece, and I'll tell you who they are," she said, pointing to silver frames where the boys were shown quite small, Billy with a tricycle and the other two with their fairy cycles. Kevin brought them across and she explained who they were, and the year. To Kevin it seemed positively history. One by one she asked him to bring her the various photographs while she sat regally in her wing armchair, keeping her back stiff and straight, not yielding to fatigue. When she got to the war and the boys in their uniforms her hand shook a little. She explained how Harry and Jack had died.

"To make the world safe for future generations. For freedom. For you," she told Kevin. "That's why they died. Was it worth it?" She handed him the last photograph, shaking her head over the world as much as Kevin.

"I've a right to live my own life," said Kevin.

"You've a duty to use it properly. Not to — to do things which make the police look for you," she said.

"They couldn't pin anything on me," said Kevin. "Got no proof." He swaggered across the room, so thin and puny to Mrs Anderson, whose boys were all tall and sturdy. "Did they all die, then?" he asked.

"Not Billy. He went to Australia. He's coming back," she said. "I'm expecting him any day now." If the youth thought Billy was due, it might frighten him off.

"He's not. He's dead too," said Kevin. "You write to him and he doesn't get the letters." He pulled open a drawer of her desk and took a handful of letters out, scattering them round the room. ''See? He's dead too,'' he said on a crowing note.

Mrs Anderson felt the flutter start up in her chest again and she wanted to snatch up the returned letters and put them away, but at the moment she had not enough strength to get up from her chair. No one had ever told her Billy was dead. He wasn't; she knew it. At first, some years ago, a lot of letters had come back, but now they were seldom returned; he was often away from home, that was all. She refused to consider that new or changing tenants of his flat would soon grow tired of dealing with his mail.

But he never wrote to her, and the cheques she sent were never cashed.

After a little while she spoke.

''Well, I see you've found my secret,'' she said. ''Why don't you tell me yours?''

But Kevin wouldn't.

CHAPTER
EIGHTEEN

When Howard returned after taking Mrs Anderson home, Muriel was in the kitchen unloading the plates and cutlery used for lunch from the dishwasher before filling it again with the tea things.

"Hours of drudgery for a meal soon over and the same thing all over again," he said, and began to help her.

"It's not drudgery when everyone enjoys it," Muriel said. Her face was flushed with effort and pleasure.

"I'm glad you asked Mrs Anderson," said Howard. "She must be rather lonely. A game old girl. What about a drink?" he added as she closed the dishwasher.

"I seem to have had plenty already today," said Muriel. "But I wouldn't say no."

She smiled at him, and for a moment under the plump cheeks and high colouring he saw the slim, earnest girl he had married so long ago. Muriel was only twenty when they met; she was a secretary in a charity organization for which his firm did the legal work. She was efficient and eager even then, convinced of the importance of the charity, which worked with handicapped children, impatient of red tape and protocol. She hadn't really changed, except to put on weight and acquire grey hair. He knew she had never thought of another man, in a sexual sense, since they married, and never would, and he stifled the thought that probably no other man had ever wanted to put temptation in her way.

He held her hand as they went back to the sitting-room, and kissed her before he poured their drinks. Muriel was surprised, but she was pleased too. For once, there was time for dalliance; she wasn't going anywhere.

Emily would not stay to supper with Janet and Laura after driving them home because it was snowing, but she came in for a glass of sherry. When she left, large flakes were falling and her tyres left deep tracks. Laura hoped it would snow all night.

"Can I go tobogganing tomorrow?" she asked.

"Daddy's coming to take you to *Peter Pan*," Janet reminded her.

"He won't be able to, if it's snowing," said Laura.

"Well — it may stop," said Janet, going to the window. The wind was rising, and the snow had begun to whirl about in a satisfactory manner. She would be the last to lament if Desmond couldn't get out of London.

"I'd rather go tobogganing," said Laura.

"Yes." But Laura's wishes couldn't prevail. Janet thought of the years ahead when this conversation would be repeated and when Laura would be compelled to visit her father, enduring the nausea of car journeys, and the likelihood that Pam, whom Laura had described to her, was only one in a succession of stepmother figures who would enter her life. If Desmond had real affection for the child it would be different, but Janet was sure he had very little. He knew insisting on access upset Janet; and Laura was a pretty, well-behaved little girl whom it was agreeable to produce; if she were plain, or became rebellious as she grew older, he might take a different line. Or perhaps, in time, Laura would be won over by the treats he provided. Janet sighed. It would never really end, or not until Laura grew up. A marriage might be over but its consequences lasted for a lifetime.

Parked motor-cycles were examined to see if among them was one registered in the name of Kevin Timms, and sundry checks were made all over the country on those being ridden. A few unlicensed ones were discovered, and two thefts, but nothing else resulted. Detective Chief Inspector Sprockett returned to his office in the evening, after a cheerful Christmas dinner, to see what had come in on the search for the missing youth, but there seemed to be no lead at all.

Before going home, he went round to the Greens' house. Marilyn's parents had only just returned from their day's work at the Rose and Crown, which had ended with several rounds of drinks for the staff. Ena was tired after a long day. During the lull between lunch and the evening she'd sat in the snug with her feet up; it wasn't worth coming home. Fred had snoozed by the fire. She'd got a little weepy when they reached home, but it was only because her legs ached, she told Fred as he poured her a port from the bottle Mrs Crow had given them. But she did miss Marilyn, she added; the girl would be making tea for them now, cutting sandwiches for a late snack. It was a shame.

It seemed appropriate when the doorbell rang and the late caller proved to be the chief inspector.

Ena dried her tears and offered him a glass of port, which Sprockett refused. He accompanied her into the front room where Fred was sitting on the torn sofa, a pile of *Sporting Life* at his feet, his face flushed and his wispy hair on end.

"Being Christmas, it makes our loss the sadder," Ena explained, repeating sentiments expressed earlier by others.

"She was such a good little girl, when she was a kiddy," Fred said. "Ever so obedient. Beats me how she came to go wrong."

"She didn't go wrong," said Sprockett. "She was a good girl."

"She can't have been," said Fred. "Having some fellow in here — "

"She was always reading them magazines. Books don't do you a bit of good, I always said to her," said Ena.

"Did she ever mention the name Kevin Timms?" Sprockett asked.

"No," Ena shook her head.

A hiccup came from Fred.

"Is that who done it, then?" he asked.

"We want to talk to him, to see if he can help with our inquiries," said Sprockett. "You don't know him?"

"Never heard of him," said Fred.

"Why don't you get on with it, then?" asked Ena

truculently. ''What's stopping you?''

''He's gone missing,'' said Sprockett. ''I wondered if you knew any of his friends.''

''Well, we don't,'' said Ena. ''You get on and find him.'' Just fancy! Marilyn had a real flesh-and-blood fellow after all! It took some getting used to: how could she be so sly?

''Oh, we will,'' said Sprockett. He stood up to go, a burly man in a tweed jacket and the dark trousers of the best suit he had worn for dinner, and Ena followed him into the narrow hallway where there was a smell of stale food. The gas company had checked the safety of the supply and presumably Ena had done as much as she planned in the way of cleaning. It was not Sprockett's intention to advise them about insurance; very likely they had none. To this drab house Marilyn had come that night, and perhaps she had invited Kevin in; that could explain how she forgot her key and left it in the door. He certainly hadn't broken in. What had she expected to happen? She was an innocent girl; an ignorant, vulnerable girl; a virgin whose body had yielded its secrets only to the doctor but whose reputation would soon be tarnished by gossip.

Ena opened the door and Sprockett went off to his car without another word; there were parents worse than the Greens. He thought of the boy they were seeking, and what was known about him; he'd had a very different sort of home, though the houses were much the same size. Allington was a bigger place with a more mixed population than Framingham; Kevin Timms' aunt tried hard with him, doing her best with unpromising material. Suppose the young people's positions had been reversed, and Marilyn had lived with the somewhat repressed, rather prim Jessie Swales, while Kevin grew up with the slatternly Greens? What would have happened to them then?

Marilyn might have survived, Sprockett thought, driving carefully home through the whirling snow.

The wind went on rising. It howled round the corner of the big house on Hatch Hill, sweeping across the fields from the north-east. Until recently, a row of elms had broken the worst of the weather from that quarter, but they had succumbed to disease and Mrs Anderson's farmer neighbour had cut them all down in the summer. At a particularly piercing banshee wail, she saw Kevin wince.

"Don't you like the wind?" she asked.

"Don't mind it," said Kevin, but he had never lived in so exposed a spot, buffeted by its full force. Jessie's house was snug among the rows of others that sheltered it, and so had been the home of his childhood. On the bike, the wind was a menace, catching your body and threatening to tip you over, an enemy.

He put on the television set, and turned up the volume to mask the eerie sound. There was a film on, in black and white, Bing Crosby singing. It must be a very old film, Mrs Anderson thought; she wouldn't recognize anyone modern but Bing had been a star in the ascendant when her own boys were young and she had rather liked him herself. Snow was falling in the film. Kevin muttered at it and tried the other channels but they had nothing he liked better. He twiddled the controls, complaining because the film was not in colour. Bing's face went fuzzy and was lost, then reappeared. Mrs Anderson wondered if the youth had any sort of plan. Suppose she suggested they had a drink? He'd already finished the bottle of sherry he'd taken to the kitchen but there were two more in the cupboard. Who had the harder head? If he got drunk, he might pass out, though what she could do about it if he did, in a blizzard and with no telephone, she was not sure.

Raising her voice above the television, she said, "There's sherry in the cupboard. Would you like some?"

"Eh?" Kevin started up. He'd been trying to get the hang of the story on the screen.

"Sherry," Mrs Anderson repeated. "Would you like some? In the cupboard." She pointed.

"Sure." Kevin fetched a bottle and, ignoring Mrs Anderson's graceful old sherry glasses, took out a tumbler, as he had before, filling it with Harvey's Amontillado.

"Thank you." Mrs Anderson held out her hand as he raised the glass to his lips.

For a moment she thought he was going to throw it at her, but he didn't. After a pause he thrust it out and she took it quickly, before he dropped it, spilling a little on the front of her dress. She'd sip it, calculating that he'd drink the rest of the bottle.

It worked out that way, and Kevin fell asleep before the television programme ended for the night. Mrs

Anderson's legs were wobbly as she rose to turn the set off. She gathered up the letters to Billy which still lay on the floor and put them away in the desk. She left one lamp burning, and the heater on, and went quietly out of the room, closing the door softly. Kevin did not stir.

Mrs Anderson walked along the passage to the front door and opened it, closing it again quickly as snow blew towards her from the bitter night outside. She knew she had not the strength to walk even to the end of the drive in such weather. She left the door on the Yale, not bolting it as she normally did, and went upstairs to the big front bedroom where she turned on the light. Shivering with cold, she switched it on and off, three short and then three longer bursts of light, and three more short ones, S O S in Morse, over and over again. Someone across the valley might look out and see it, she thought forlornly, even someone in a plane above. She forgot that the blizzard would hide the house from any plane, and even shorten visibility close to. She stayed there, flashing the light, until she was too cold to endure it any more. Then she went along to her bedroom, boiled the kettle for her hot water bottle, and prepared for bed, locking the door.

She tried to pretend that Billy would arrive next day, and rescue her. Mercifully, after some time, she fell into an exhausted, rather restless sleep.

CHAPTER
NINETEEN

By morning four inches of snow had fallen over southern England and a good deal more in Scotland and the north. The wind had blown it into drifts which blocked roads and lanes, and snowploughs were out trying to keep main routes clear. As soon as they passed, the strong wind blew the snow back to block them again.

Detective Chief Inspector Sprockett had to dig his way out of his drive before he could leave for the office. Detective Sergeant Crisp left his car at home and walked. Because it was Boxing Day, traffic was light everywhere, but calls were already coming into Allington Central Police Station reporting cars in ditches and roads impassable. Even so, constables living in rural areas were ordered to check farms and barns in the hunt for Kevin Timms, though Sprockett felt sure he must have left the district. A message warned that he might be violent but was probably not armed. However, the saving of life in the blizzard was more immediately important than apprehending Timms, and a thorough search could not be mounted until the weather improved. Officers in cars on patrol or aiding snowbound motorists were told to make sure he wasn't hiding in any isolated buildings they might pass.

He could be lodging somewhere, openly staying in a boarding house or digs. Sprockett obtained divisional consent for a broadcast description to go out on various radio wavelengths.

Janet telephoned Desmond at half-past eight that morning. He sounded cross and sleepy, and she wondered if he'd had a thick night and whether she'd roused him from the arms of Pamela.

"We've got a lot of snow here and the roads are blocked," she told him, exaggerating, but she'd rung Emily first to see how things were at her end of the village. Emily always woke early, and she good-naturedly offered to put on her boots and walk to the end of the road to inspect what lay beyond. She rang back to report thick drifts on the roads out of Framingham and said no traffic had gone through that morning; what there was on the by-pass seemed to be moving very slowly and she thought there was only one lane open. Her opinion was that anyone who set out by car today, unless he really had to, was a lunatic.

Desmond said that there was very little snow in London and he didn't want to disappoint Laura.

"Even if you get here, you may not be able to bring her back," Janet pointed out. "You may have to keep her till the thaw. Snow's always worse in the country, Desmond."

"She could come by train."

"The services are bound to be disrupted by the weather. Besides, I'm not sure there are any trains today," said Janet. And she certainly wasn't letting

Laura go by train alone, anywhere, at her age. "It's still snowing," she added, as a few sparse flakes drifted past the window.

"Hold on," said Desmond, and the telephone went mute as he muffled it, presumably to confer with Pamela. Soon he came back on the line.

"Very well. I'll be in touch," he said. "But I don't know if I'll be able to get rid of the tickets."

Janet knew it was the argument that he might get stuck with Laura that had won the day.

Kevin woke with a thumping headache and a sour taste in his mouth. At first he couldn't remember where he was. He expected to see the shape of his own wardrobe in the corner, and the walls he'd painted orange; then he remembered the attic, but that wasn't right either; he wasn't in bed. He lay fully dressed on a small, rather hard sofa in a dim-lit room, and as he realized it was Mrs Anderson's sitting-room, the paraffin heater, with a few popping sounds, expired.

The old crow! Where was she? Had she got away and gone for the fuzz? Kevin sprang up and rushed to the door, which he expected to find locked, but it wasn't. He bounded up the stairs, two at a time, and along the passage to Mrs Anderson's room, flinging the door open. The bed was neatly made and there was no sign of her. Heart in throat, he raced down again and opened the front door. Snow whirled at him, making him step backwards. He peered out. There were no footprints, but she might have gone hours ago. He banged the door shut. They'd be coming for him any minute. Snow wouldn't stop the fuzz. He raced upstairs to get his keys. He'd have a job with the bike in this. Glancing out of the landing window, he saw snow covering everything, blown into heaps against trees and leaving bare their branches. He'd never seen so much of the stuff.

He clattered downstairs and as he arrived in the hall the kitchen door at the end of the passage opened. Kevin picked up the chair that stood near the front door, holding it before him like a shield, but it was no uniformed pig who emerged from the kitchen, just the old crone, wearing a flowered apron.

She looked at him steadily, realizing that the chair was for use as a weapon.

"Breakfast's ready," she said calmly, and turned back into the kitchen.

Kevin took several seconds, after putting the chair down, to recover poise enough to strut confidently into the kitchen. The table was laid with a blue and white checked cloth. There was a fresh square of butter in a dish. There were large cups and saucers, white with a blue and gold pattern, and plates to match. There was toast in a silver rack, and a pot of honey. As he came towards the table, Mrs Anderson set down a delicately painted china teapot. Then she went to the Aga, stooped to the low oven and brought out two plates. She put one at the place laid where Kevin had sat the night before. On it were two fried eggs, some crisp rashers of bacon, and two pieces of fried bread cut into triangles. There was a clean table-napkin beside Kevin's place. She had not prepared her usual porridge the night before and had cooked one egg and a single rasher for herself, on the principle she had already adopted of maintaining her strength and her position. She took off her apron, hung it up and sat down, taking her own table-napkin from its silver ring and laying it on her lap.

She poured out two cups of tea and passed one to Kevin. Silently, he took it from her.

''Do you take sugar?'' she asked, and when he nodded, offered him the bowl. It was lump sugar, and there were tongs in the bowl. Kevin fumbled with them, putting four lumps into his tea. He'd never seen such things before.

Mrs Anderson began to eat her own breakfast. Kevin attempted his, but he felt rather sick and didn't really want it. After a few mouthfuls he got up and rushed out of the room. He closed no doors and Mrs Anderson could hear him being sick in the downstairs lavatory. It was not surprising after all that sherry. She hoped he'd managed to get all the way in time. She went on with her own breakfast, washing it down with plenty of tea. She'd thought again about putting aspirins in his; it would have been easy, this morning. But he might notice the taste. He'd liked the sherry and there was still another bottle. There was also the rest of the brandy, a bottle of whisky, and two bottles of claret she'd had for a long time with never an occasion worth opening them. It would probably be easy enough to persuade him to join her in a drink, later in the day when he'd recovered and the weather might have moderated.

Before preparing breakfast, she had taken the charred remains of her fur stole out to the bootroom, and left it there in the pail, and, despite the cold, she opened the kitchen window briefly to blow away the smell of smoke.

On Boxing Day morning, Police Constable Frewen helped a motorist dig his car out of a fresh snow drift on a hill between Framingham and Allington where it was blocking the road, delaying other travellers including Dr Baynes on his way to an urgent case. The wind still blew in strong gusts and the road would soon be blocked again. Frewen followed the doctor to make sure he reached the main road safely. Dr Baynes drove cautiously; he, at least, would respect the conditions and not belt along like a maniac, Frewen thought as he saw the Peugeot turn into the main road. Dr Baynes should be all right now; Frewen had driven that way earlier and the snow had packed down hard after the passage of the plough and the subsequent traffic. It was the minor roads, which the gritting lorry had not reached, that were the worst.

Frewen drove on to the by-pass and cruised along it slowly. The gritting lorry went past on the other carriageway, but there was not enough traffic to turn the melting snow in its wake into slush. There would be more later, when holidaymakers headed home, and then the trouble would really begin, with visibility poor in the dark and idiots racing along as if it were a summer's day. Frewen saw a barn in a field at the side of the road and pulled into the side. He was already wearing his rubber boots, and he plodded through deep snow to the gate, which was padlocked. There were no tracks in the snow leading to the barn, but if Timms were inside, his footsteps would have long since been obliterated. Frewen climbed the gate and trudged on to the barn, his collar turned up against the weather, his cap pulled low.

The barn was a solid structure with wooden doors secured by a bar on the outside. The youth could not have shut the door upon himself, but all the same Frewen opened it and searched inside. There were a few hay bales and a harrow; nothing else. He secured the door and plodded back to his car.

Further on, where the by-pass went under the bridge leading to the church, there was a tiny patch of road free of snow. Frewen came to the turn to Hatch Hill. The snow plough had been along, and as he paused at the foot of the hill the gritting lorry swung past him and turned up. Frewen reported his whereabouts on the radio and said he was going behind it to make sure the way was clear and the road to Dartworth open.

Driving slowly behind the lorry, Frewen came to the entrance to The Gables. Snow had blown in great drifts across the gateway, and the wind was bending the trees that bordered the drive. Even with grit fresh on the road, Frewen thought that if he stopped now, he might not be able to get the car moving on the hill, but this was certainly an isolated house. He had not forgotten the sight of that poor girl's body, and he wanted to hear that Kevin Timms had been found. He drove on to the first crossroads, turned the car and ran gently back downhill to The Gables again. He passed no other dwelling.

He took his shovel with him up the drive, but he did

not have to use it to cleave his way, skirting the deepest drifts. He made no sound.

Kevin, emerging from the shed where he had gone for paraffin for the stove, felt his heart lurch with terror when he saw the figure of the policeman, a shovel over his shoulder, not fifty yards away.

''Hey — you all right there?'' Frewen called.

What he saw was a youth with a checked scarf wound round his neck and a tweed cap on his head, his body encased in a large burberry-type raincoat. The style of the peaked cap was now fashionable again in a certain set, having been *de rigueur* long before when Billy Anderson was young. Kevin wore a pair of old sheepskin gloves he'd found in the cloakroom, and some rubber boots. Very little of his face was visible, and none of his hair.

He had been too paralysed with shock to flee.

''Not seen any strangers up here, have you?'' the policeman was calling.

''No — no, I haven't,'' said Kevin.

''Who lives here?'' Frewen asked. He took a step forward.

Kevin hesitated, and the policeman advanced further.

''My — my grandmother,'' Kevin said, inspired.

''And who's she?''

''Mrs Anderson — that's her name,'' said Kevin, and his heart thumped as the policeman moved closer.

''And what's yours?'' Frewen asked.

Kevin thought wildly.

''Billy,'' he said. ''Billy Anderson. That's my name. I'm just visiting.''

190

"That's lucky for your gran, then," said Frewen.

"Yeah," agreed Kevin. "She's okay. I'm looking after her."

"Right," said Frewen. "Terrible weather, isn't it?" he added cheerfully, and he plodded off.

Kevin stumbled into the house, sick with panic. He'd locked the old woman up while he fetched the paraffin, taken her up to her bedroom and shut her inside, telling her he'd let her out when it was time to get his dinner ready. He'd thought about making her fetch the paraffin herself — she'd have had to, if he wasn't there; then he realized he'd have to go outside too, standing over her while she got it, and it would all take much longer.

Mrs Anderson had not told him that there were two spare cans of paraffin in the bootroom, left there by thoughtful Joe Knox who liked to feel she need not go out for it if the weather was bad, though he lectured her against keeping too much in the house. She'd hoped, if the boy went out of the house, that she might be able to prevent him returning by locking the doors against him, though he would probably only break his way back in through a window.

She heard voices as she sat in the armchair in her room, and levered herself up to look out of the window, but by the time she got there, the caller was leaving. Mrs Anderson made out the uniformed figure of a policeman departing down the drive. By the time she had opened the window to call to him, he was out of sight, and she knew that the wind would carry away any cry she might make.

Somehow she closed the window and stumbled back to

her chair. It was almost too much to bear. Some minutes passed before she began to wonder why the policeman had come to the house at all; not to look for this youth, anyway, or he would have been arrested. But she was sure he had committed a crime for he had implied, the night before, that the police might want him.

At first she'd refused to go upstairs, when he'd ordered her to, and then he'd threatened to lock her in the cellar. It had seemed better to give in; she'd very soon be chilled through in the cellar, and in her own room, besides being warm, she felt less of a prisoner.

Some time after the policeman had gone she heard him moving round the house and then the sound of water running in her bathroom. He was having a bath! What impertinence, she thought at first, astonished that he bothered. But he had looked clean and spruce; his singlet, when she first saw him, was spotless. It was the fluff on his chin and his lank hair that made him look unkempt.

He might kill her, she thought calmly. She was not afraid of death, only of the manner of dying. This young hooligan was more afraid than she was and therein lay her peril, for if she upset him he might panic. It would be degrading to meet death at his hands.

He took a long time over his bath.

Later, he released her, his hair freshly washed and still damp, wearing a clean shirt. He'd been going to tell her to wash his other one, but in the end it had seemed less trouble to do it himself. She was safe enough in her room. Good thing she hadn't seen that copper, though.

He told her about it after lunch, when they had the

chicken, which she had put in a casserole with carrots, onions and potatoes. Afterwards there was custard.

"Do you like custard?" she had asked him. "My boys used to love it, with jam."

So did Kevin.

How long would this strange dialogue between her and the youth go on? Neither Joe Knox nor the laundryman were due for nearly two weeks, nor even Mrs Clarke.

When he had finished his custard, she washed up. Testing him, she handed him a tea towel.

"Don't you help at home?" she asked.

"If I want to," said Kevin. In spite of himself, he picked up a spoon and began wiping it. It was very shiny.

"Where do you live?" Mrs Anderson asked.

"Nowhere. Yes — here," he said.

"Where did you live before you came here?"

"With my auntie," said Kevin.

The diminutive sounded odd on his lips.

"My mum — she's dead," Kevin went on.

"I'm very sorry. That's sad," said Mrs Anderson. She laid a plate on the drainer for him to dry.

"It was long ago," said Kevin.

"I expect you miss her," said Mrs Anderson. She said no more until they had finished the dishes, and then she suggested, "Shall we go into the other room? I've got some chocolates. I was given them yesterday for Christmas. Wouldn't it be nice to have one?"

"I don't mind," said Kevin.

The sitting-room was warm. Kevin had filled the heater and adjusted the wick; he seemed to understand it. Mrs Anderson took the box of chocolates from a drawer and pulled off the cellophane wrapping.

"Which ones do you like?" she asked, pulling out the printed guide to the different centres.

"I like the hard ones," said Kevin.

"Now isn't that lucky, because I like soft ones," said Mrs Anderson.

Kevin almost smiled.

"You could say so," he said.

Mrs Anderson took a coffee cream and put the box where Kevin could easily reach it. Then she settled into her chair.

"Was your mother ill for long?" she asked.

"She wasn't ill. It was a fire," said Kevin and his glance strayed to the paraffin heater. A hard expression came over his face. Mrs Anderson remembered the fate of her fur stole and had a new awareness of danger. She said nothing. For minutes the boy gazed at the fire, far away in thought. Then suddenly sat up, took another chocolate, and while he chewed it said, "A pig came here today."

"A pig?" Mrs Anderson was puzzled.

"A pig — a rozzer — a policeman," said Kevin impatiently. He grinned then, a crafty grin. "He was asking if there'd been any strangers about. He was looking for me, most likely." It was the fire that had set them on to him, Kevin reasoned. Bob Watson would put the blame on him fast enough. He'd not thought of that, before.

"What did you tell him?" Mrs Anderson asked carefully.

"Oh, I said we hadn't seen anyone," said Kevin. "I

told him I was your grandson, Billy Anderson, like you told me about your son what's in Australia. Him that's dead. His son, like." He preened himself, proud of his deceit.

Mrs Anderson was silent. She had not thought him capable of such swift improvisation.

"What is your real name?" she asked at last.

Kevin told her.

"I see," she said. "And why was the policeman looking for you?" Would she learn, now, what he had done?

Kevin considered. He took another chocolate. The bath this morning, and the change of clothes, had made him feel much better and his headache was quite gone. It wasn't too bad, sitting here with this old dame, passing the time. He'd been getting bored up there in the attic, though it was snug enough. They were safe now, for a policeman had seen for himself that nothing was wrong and if anyone else called, the grandson dodge would work again. He could always force the old cow to agree that he was her grandson by a pinch or a twist of her arm.

"The police don't know it was me that did the other," said Kevin, ignoring her question.

"What other?"

"The girl."

"Which girl?"

"In the paper, it was. Marilyn, that was her name. Silly fat cow," said Kevin. "Shouldn't have hurt her, a bump like that. Banged her head, she did."

"Marilyn Green," said Mrs Anderson, keeping her voice steady.

"That's right. She was stupid."

Mrs Anderson looked across at him as he sat there, swinging one leg, still looking at the fire. So this was the youth mentioned by Mrs Clarke, the one who had got into the house, for whatever reason, and attacked poor Marilyn. He looked too puny. But he'd talked about her as the other: had he killed someone else?

"People have to do what I want," Kevin said in a harsh voice, sitting upright in the chair and staring at her. "Don't you forget that."

"I see," said Mrs Anderson quietly. "And what do you want to do now, Kevin? Would you like to play cards? I often play patience."

"What's that?" Kevin asked suspiciously.

"A card game for one person. I'll show you, if you like."

They played cards for nearly two hours. First Mrs Anderson showed him various forms of patience and then she taught him Beggar My Neighbour. It was just the right level for him, she decided. By managing not to notice every time payment was due to her, she contrived for him to win each game. She knew that Kevin would be a bad loser.

CHAPTER
TWENTY

Next morning the wind dropped and the sun came out.
There had been a severe frost during the night and the
snow was crystalline, sparkling against the bright
blue of the sky. Pandora was opening today, so when the
mother of Jenny, Laura's friend, telephoned suggesting
she should take the two little girls tobogganing on Hatch
Hill, Janet gratefully agreed.

Snug in anorak and trousers, a scarlet knitted cap on
her head, feet in two pairs of socks in her wellington
boots, Laura set off for Jenny's house, which was in the
next road, towing her toboggan behind her. When she
arrived, Jenny's mother was still washing up breakfast,
but soon she was ready and with the two small girls, and
her son Giles, who was seven, set off through the town
and over the bridge across the by-pass to the church.
They dragged the toboggans through the churchyard,
past graves where wreaths laid for Christmas were
covered in snow. In a far corner lay the unmarked grave
of Marilyn Green, with one faded, snow-covered spray
of bronze chrysanthemums frozen stiff. Over a stile at
the end of the churchyard went the little party, and along
a footpath to the fields. The snow was already churned
up by other tobogganers ahead of them. Jenny's mother

stumped along with the children, her fair hair tied in a pony-tail that flopped against her anorak. Their way led along the ridge across more stiles until finally they reached the road at the foot of Hatch Hill. They crossed it, climbed a gate because they could not open it against the weight of snow, passing the toboggans over, and then began the climb up the back of the hill. They could hear the shouts of those who had arrived earlier and soon figures careered towards them as they climbed. At the top of the hill, beyond the start to their run, no longer screened by trees because the dead elms had been cut down, was the only house in sight, The Gables.

Jenny's mother stayed watching them for some time as they made their descents. Then Giles began to complain because snow had got inside his boots and melted, making his feet cold. She took him home, instructing the two little girls to start back no later than half-past twelve. They both wore watches — Jenny's had been new for Christmas — so there could be no excuse for forgetting the time.

Muriel dialled Mrs Anderson's number again that morning. The line had been dead the day before when she rang to see if the old lady was all right after the heavy fall of snow in the night; clearly the blizzard had put the telephone out or order but Muriel had been unable to report it because the Faults department was not working over the holiday. It was still dead. Muriel rang Faults again and this time obtained a response. A pleasant voice agreed to look into it but said there was a lot of trouble due to the weather. Muriel explained that the subscriber was an old lady living alone, and Faults, who seemed full of the Christmas spirit, promised to see what could be done.

"She's probably quite cosy and snug," Muriel had said to Howard. "Her little sitting-room gets nice and warm and she's got plenty of food. She must be used to being housebound when the weather's bad."

Muriel's own day was to be busy with a children's party at a hall near Allington. She had jellies and sandwiches to prepare herself, and would be at the party all the afternoon.

"Be careful driving, won't you, dear?" Howard said, kissing her fondly before leaving for his train. "Enjoy your day."

The police had checked a number of isolated farms, barns and derelict buildings all over the country on Boxing Day, in their search for Kevin Timms. On Wednesday, though the main roads in the Allington area were all open, many minor ones were blocked and others were very icy. There was a crop of accidents in the morning when shops reopened and people went back to work, but most factories were closed until the new year and that reduced peak-hour traffic. Police Constable Frewen's visit to the barn and to The Gables were in his report. A youth who looked like Timms had been picked up in Birmingham but was released when able to prove his own identity. Door-to-door inquiries began in Allington, and, because the youth had worked in Framingham and the dead girl lived there, in Framingham too.

No one seemed to know Kevin well. A constable spoke to the personnel manager of the factory where he had worked before being made redundant; he supplied the names of other youths who had worked in the same part of the factory. Two were out when the police called; the others agreed that they knew Kevin because they worked together, but they had never met him outside the factory. One mentioned that he liked tinkering with his motor-bike. He never went to rallies or scrambles, as far as they knew. His last employer, Dave Blewett at the garage, said he was surly at work and on poor terms with the rest of the staff. Money had gone from the till, and a helmet out of stock; such things had not happened before Kevin Timms was taken on.

He'd need money. The cash he'd taken from his aunt would soon run out and he might try theft. Reports of break-ins and robberies must be investigated bearing this in mind. The Christmas period had been peaceful in this respect and the snow would hinder thieves: it was too easy to leave tracks.

Detective Constable Mitchell called on Jessie, who had the week off. Kevin had not attempted to get in touch with her; there had been no letter, no telephone call.

The police did not tell her they had found a brand-new nylon nightdress among his belongings. They did not know he had bought it for her. It was just another item in their list of imponderables about Kevin Timms.

It was still dark when Mrs Anderson woke on Wednesday morning. Kevin had drunk a tumbler of sherry the evening before but after that had moved on to tea; Mrs Anderson had brewed three pots before they went to bed.

"Sickly stuff, that. Gets you after a bit," he'd said of the sherry.

Mrs Anderson had managed another tot of brandy for herself in secret; she laced one of her cups of tea, too. It helped her to keep going. They had thick farmhouse soup from a tin for supper, and bread and cheese, and Kevin ate the last banana. They'd eaten the Christmas cake at about five. Kevin wanted to play cards again after that. Mrs Anderson showed him the few tricks she knew — she thought she had forgotten them but they came back to her — and then she taught him Pelmanism. By playing slowly and carefully she let him win each game yet took a few pairs herself. There was a pop programme on the television and he watched that, which gave her a rest, but the raucous noise of electronic music and the shouting voices seemed to pierce her head and it was all she could do to sit through it without complaint.

In a lull, she said she was tired and was going to bed.

"Go ahead, then," said Kevin, his eyes on the screen.

She went, quietly, and from the front bedroom signalled S O S with the light once more, for a long time.

Kevin came up to lock her into her bedroom but she had already locked the door from the inside. When he rattled it, she called out, "Good night, Kevin. I hope you sleep."

Of course he'd sleep. Didn't he always?

But that night he woke often, his sheets in a tangle, pulse racing, a series of images echoing in his mind's eye — flames, Marilyn's scared, bewildered face, and then his mother, and the sound of screams filled his head.

The screams were his own, and when he realized that, he sat up in bed waiting for someone — anyone — the old woman — to comfort him. But no one came.

No one heard. Mrs Anderson's room was too far away.

In the morning, Kevin was the first down. There was no sound from Mrs Anderson's bedroom as he paused on the landing. Maybe she'd died in the night. Well, so what? He went on downstairs and put the kettle on to boil. He got out the frying pan and took bacon and three eggs from the larder. If she hadn't come when they were ready, he'd eat hers. He felt very hungry after his wakeful night and he'd have fancied some cornflakes first, but she hadn't got any. He'd asked her why not, and she'd said oatmeal porridge made overnight in the Aga was the only cereal she ate. She'd put a pan in the oven the evening before.

Mrs Anderson came into the kitchen just as he was taking the fried eggs out of the pan. Because her entry gave him a fright, he broke the egg he was lifting and cursed as the streaming yolk poured on to the plate.

''Now look what you've made me do,'' he said.

''Never mind, it'll taste just the same,'' said Mrs Anderson placidly. ''I'll lay the table while you make the tea.'' And calmly she took the cloth from the drawer and spread it over the table, setting out cutlery and china. ''The porridge will be ready, Kevin,'' she said.

"It just needs a stir. Mind you don't burn yourself on the pan."

Meekly, Kevin took the porridge pan out of the low oven and put the plates of egg and bacon in it to keep hot. Mrs Anderson took two bowls from the side of the stove where she'd left them to warm overnight, with the teapot. She spooned smooth, hot porridge into the bowls and was reminded of Goldilocks and the three bears. Had Kevin ever heard the story of that other intruder?

"Are you going to have salt on your porridge?" she asked. "That's the Scots way. My boys never liked it — they preferred syrup."

Kevin had never tried syrup on porridge. He found it was nice and almost smiled at her as he ate it. His soft beard was quite noticeable now, downy fluff, gingery in colour, fuzzing his chin, much fairer than his hair. It and the skimpy moustache changed his appearance. In another week his own aunt wouldn't recognize him, Mrs Anderson thought.

They finished the milk at breakfast.

"When does he come, your milkman?" Kevin asked. "Ours comes about six."

"He's late here," said Mrs Anderson. "Not till eleven or so."

"Get some extra," Kevin ordered.

"Yes," agreed Mrs Anderson. The milkman came only every other day under her arrangements with him, for a pint of milk lasted her two days; he left two pints on Saturdays. Could she put a note out asking him to send the police?

"Write out a note," Kevin went on. "Say your

grandson's staying. I'll put it out with the bottles''
Where d'you leave it?''

"On the back step.''

Wouldn't the milkman think the message strange? Surely people just asked for an extra pint, not explaining? She tried to think of a way to code a warning but could think of none. In the end she simply wrote *Grandson visiting. Two pints please.* Kevin stuck the paper in the empty bottle and put it outside the back door. Then he put her radio on and tuned it to Radio Two. When the programme was interrupted for the news headlines they were washing up and both heard the announcer say that police in Herts were anxious to interview Kevin Timms, aged nineteen, in connection with the death of Marilyn Green. He was described, and the clothes he might be wearing; and his motor-cycle number was given. Listeners were warned that the youth was not thought to be armed but might be violent. The broadcast ended with the telephone number of Allington Central Police Station.

Mrs Anderson went on scrubbing away at the porridge pan, making no comment.

"I'm not violent,'' Kevin said, in the tone of a small child falsely accused of a misdemeanour.

Mrs Anderson remained silent.

"I'm not,'' Kevin insisted. "I haven't been violent to you, have I?''

"You twisted my arm, and you struck me,'' said Mrs Anderson.

"That's not violent. That's just showing you who's boss,'' Kevin said.

"And you were just showing that girl who was boss?"

"That's right. How was I to know she'd snuff it?"

Mrs Anderson wondered how he'd killed her. Throttled her?

"It's not fair, me getting the blame," Kevin went on petulantly. "It was her fault." And who'd put the finger on him? How did the fuzz know? Someone had described him to them, and his clothes. Jessie? Wait till he saw her; he'd teach her a lesson all right. "You can't trust people," he said.

Mrs Anderson did not answer. For the first time she began to think, not just of escaping, but of persuading him to give himself up. People were very eager, nowadays, to spare offenders, heedless of their victims, and he might be dealt with more leniently if he surrendered — not that he deserved any lenience for what he had done to that unfortunate girl. There was some mystery surrounding his mother's death; his expression, when he talked about it, had given Mrs Anderson a moment of fear: that, and the burning of her fur, had been the worst times since she found him in the attic.

She folded the tablecloth and put it away in a drawer of the dresser. The drawer was tidy; there were other cloths there and a pile of table napkins.

"You can see everything in it," Kevin remarked, breaking the silence. "Just like my auntie's. That Marilyn — her place was a tip."

"I like things orderly," said Mrs Anderson.

"I do too," said Kevin. "You and me's a bit alike."

"In what way? Because we're both tidy?" He was neat, she'd already noticed it.

"Oh, that — but we're on our own, like," Kevin said. "You here, and me."

"You have your aunt," Mrs Anderson pointed out.

"She's going to marry that fancy man of hers," said Kevin.

"Oh? Who is that?"

"Some geyser she met at work," said Kevin. "He's old."

"Well, I don't suppose your aunt is very young," said Mrs Anderson.

"She's forty-two," said Kevin.

"You should — but aren't you pleased she's getting married and will have someone to look after her?" said Mrs Anderson. She must not make statements about what Kevin should do or seem to give him commands of any sort; comment must be implied to avoid provoking him.

"I'd look after her when she got too old to work," said Kevin.

"But you'd — wouldn't you want to get married one day?"

"I don't like girls that much," said Kevin.

"Who do you like, apart from your aunt?"

Kevin shrugged.

"Do you like yourself?"

"Course. Everyone likes theirselves."

"I wouldn't like myself if it caused the death of a kind girl," said Mrs Anderson.

"She wasn't a kind girl," said Kevin. "She was a stupid, ugly cow who wouldn't — " he stopped, unable to tell this old woman what Marilyn would not do.

"She was a kind girl," repeated Mrs Anderson. "She worked at Fresh Foods, at the till, and she always helped me because she saw that I am old."

"You knew her?" There was amazement in Kevin's voice.

"I saw her every week. I miss her very much," said Mrs Anderson. "Now, I'm going into the sitting-room. Are you coming?"

Without looking at him, she walked out of the kitchen. She had lighted the heater in the sitting-room when she came downstairs and heard Kevin busy in the kitchen; it would soon need refilling since they had sat up so late again. She was already feeling very tired and was glad to sit down.

Kevin followed her.

"I'll get the cards out," he said.

"Did you play cards with Marilyn?" Mrs Anderson asked.

"Not her, no. You know I didn't hardly know any card games," Kevin said. "What're you trying to do? Trick me?" His face had gone hard and he stood above her, fists clenched.

"No, no — I forgot," said Mrs Anderson. "Old people are forgetful."

He accepted it. Slowly he relaxed.

"I'm a little tired. I'd like a little rest. Then we'll have a game," she said.

She did look a bit weird. Her lined face was very pale and had gone a funny blue round the mouth. But she was so covered in wrinkles, it was difficult to decide if she was putting it on. Kevin gave her the benefit of the doubt.

"I'll make some tea," he said.

"Thank you," she said, though they had only just finished their rather late breakfast.

She was feeling quite faint, and when he left the room she went over to the window and opened it at the bottom, breathing in the sharp, cold air. Borne across the garden towards her came the faint sound of voices. She stood there wondering who it could be and for a moment she thought it was the boys. Then she understood. Years ago, Harry, Jack and Billy had taken their toboggans, when it snowed, into the field beyond the garden and slid down Hatch Hill. This was the noise of other children disporting themselves in the snow.

They would not hear her, if she shouted. They could not help.

She closed the window. If Kevin knew they were there, he would be frightened, and then anything could happen.

Out of her sight, two small girls in woolly caps, anoraks, and wellington boots, were climbing the fence into the garden.

It was Jenny's idea.

Tugging their toboggans up the hill for yet another run, she'd said, "A witch lives in that house."

"What?" Laura stopped in her progress.

"A witch. She's got white hair and a hooky nose," said Jenny. "And casts spells on you."

Laura shut her eyes, the better to imagine Mrs Anderson's countenance. She saw wrinkles and folds, blue eyes, and a nose which, it was true, was a little beaky, though she had not thought of it like that until now.

"It's not hooky," she protested. "Not like an eagle. More an owl. And she isn't a witch." This was said with authority. "I know her."

"She is. On moonlight nights she flies out of the window on a broomstick and goes about bewitching people," said Jenny firmly.

"What to do?" asked Laura practically.

"Oh — I don't know. Making you have nightmares," said Jenny, invention failing her.

"Sounds as if you've been having nightmares," said Laura bluntly. "Have you ever seen her?"

"No. I just heard it," said Jenny vaguely. She turned to Laura, bright eyes sparkling under her yellow cap. "If you know her, let's go and visit her. I'd like to meet a witch."

"She's not a witch, and I do know her," Laura repeated. "We could, I suppose," she said, eyeing the fence separating their field from the garden of The Gables. There was an evergreen hedge beyond, but in spots it was bare, where it had died off and never been replaced. They could climb in. She'd told Mrs Anderson she would visit her.

Jenny advanced towards a gap in the fence, towing her toboggan behind her. There was wire netting along the bottom of the stout post and rails. She tied the rope of her toboggan to the bottom rail and climbed briskly over.

"Come on," she said impatiently.

"Suppose she sees us in the garden?" Laura said

doubtfully. "We're trespassing." The proper way to visit was by the front door, unless you knew the people very well.

"Oh, pooh!" said Jenny scornfully. "You said you knew her. Maybe she'll ask us in and give us some sweets."

Laura tethered her toboggan too, and slowly followed her friend into the alien ground. Keeping close together, they walked through the unmarked snow among the bare-branched small trees of the copse and then the orchard towards the house. The windows glinted in the sunlight. To the two small girls it seemed far off, separated from them by a snow-covered gulf through which thrust the withered heads of overgrown herbaceous plants, shrubs, and rose trees.

"It looks very quiet," said Jenny, her valour subsiding.

"Maybe she isn't up yet," said Laura. "She's awfully old. She probably spends most of the day in bed, like in Red Riding Hood. The grandmother."

The two little girls looked at one another, each remembering how that story had developed; then, without another word, they began to run back the way they had come, following their own tracks to the fence.

"Our toboggans!" cried Laura. "Someone may have taken them. One of those boys. We shouldn't have left them."

But their toboggans were safe, still tied to the fence.

CHAPTER
TWENTY ONE

The morning wore on. After several games of Snap, Mrs Anderson showed Kevin how to make a card house. She set two cards together, tentwise, to start them off, then balanced her structure round this central support. It was like entertaining a six-year-old. She encouraged him to take over the construction, afraid he would construe the tremor in her hand as due to fear. But when the card house collapsed, Kevin's humour changed and he started to curse. Mrs Anderson gathered up the cards and said calmly that they would try again later, and what about lunch?

She cut up the remains of the chicken and asked Kevin if he liked curry. He'd had curried prawns from a Chinese take-away, it seemed, but otherwise was uncertain.

''Well, we need something hot in this weather,'' said Mrs Anderson bracingly. She made the curry sauce, adding apple and sultanas, and put it in the oven while the rice boiled.

''Good old stove, that,'' said Kevin. ''I ain't seen one like it before.''

''It's very convenient to have the oven always ready,'' said Mrs Anderson.

She noticed his speech had lapsed and wondered what it indicated. Perhaps he had been corrected too often by his careful aunt. Had she any real affection for him or did she care for him only from a sense of duty? Duty was no substitute for love, but Kevin was scarcely endearing.

"How long have you been coming to this house?" she asked him as she laid the table.

"Let's see — November, it was. Early, like," said Kevin. "I'd stop an hour or two. Never more than that till now."

"Why did you stay this time?"

"Had to get away, didn't I? Had to show her. And him. But I done that all right." Once again the evil grin spread across his face.

What else had he done? Killed his aunt?

"How did you get in?" Mrs Anderson asked.

"Opened a window."

"But they are all shut and locked."

"It's easy to push back them locks," said Kevin. "Just use a knife, you do. I got in easy. Didn't take noth — anything."

Mrs Anderson thought of the money missing from her purse and the food that had disappeared, making her doubt her own sanity.

"S'nice up there," Kevin volunteered. "In that little room. It gets real warm and nice."

"Haven't you got a nice room at your aunt's?"

"Yeah — it was all right," said Kevin.

"What do you expect to happen?" Mrs Anderson asked, sitting down at the table. Kevin had moved to the stove and was resting with his back to its warmth, a posture she often adopted herself. ''You won't be able to stay here for ever.''

''They're looking for me now,'' said Kevin, and there was a weird sort of satisfaction in his tone. ''I can't leave here while the heat's on. In a few days or a few weeks the search will move off and then I can get away at night. Get far away.'' He spoke dreamily, his eyes half closed, seeing himself roaring into the dark on his bike, eluding the police forces of the whole country.

''What then? They won't stop looking for you. How will you live?''

''I'll take all your money with me,'' said Kevin.

''I've only a few pounds in the house. I'd have to go to the bank to get some more,'' said Mrs Anderson. ''You couldn't trust me to do that without telling the police, could you?''

''No,'' said Kevin.

''You can't stay in hiding for the rest of your life, Kevin, and you can't — '' she sought for the right expression — ''stay on the run. They'll catch you in the end. You might get a lighter sentence if you gave yourself up.''

Kevin began tapping his hand on the top of the stove.

''Cut that out,'' he said angrily. He walked over to her and lifted his hand as if he would strike her. ''You and me's been getting on all right, with the cards and that. Don't go telling me what to do.'' He repeated, ''No one tells Kevin Timms what to do.''

Mrs Anderson ignored his threatening pose.

''Why are you afraid of me, Kevin?'' she asked.

"Who'd be afraid of you? I'm not," Kevin jeered.

"You must be, or you wouldn't want to hit me," said Mrs Anderson. "I'm sure you would never have hit your mother, or your real grandmother, come to that. Do you remember her?"

He did, his maternal grandmother. She was a stout little woman with bright brown eyes. She had been very strict; he would never have dared misbehave in her presence.

"No," he said, denying her memory.

"Well, I'm sure you wouldn't have. Now, the meal should be ready. Please let me pass."

He stood aside to allow her to get to the stove, and they ate in silence, following the curry with tinned pears. When he had finished his several slices of pear, and she her single half, Kevin rose and collected the plates.

"Sorry," she heard him say gruffly, as he turned away.

Mrs Anderson felt almost light-hearted, washing up. Very few people, she was sure, had ever heard Kevin apologize.

They remembered the milk after lunch and Kevin fetched it from the back door step. It had frozen in the bottles so that over an inch stood up above the rim, the foil cap perched on top. Kevin could not remember seeing it like that before.

"There are some games in a cupboard in one of the attic rooms," Mrs Anderson said. "Other games, not card games. Snakes and ladders and Ludo." Though snakes and ladders might be a risky choice with Kevin,

214

since fortune could not be manipulated. "Would you like to play some of those this afternoon? Shall we go and see what we can find?"

"I don't mind," said Kevin.

Mrs Anderson took this for consent. They set off, Kevin walking behind her. The hall was icy, the windows rimed inside with frost. Slowly, Mrs Anderson ascended the second staircase and opened the door of the room with the toy cupboard.

"They didn't half have a lot of toys," said Kevin. "Your kids. All this stuff."

"Yes. They were lucky," said Mrs Anderson. "Those are the games." She pointed to a pile of cardboard boxes. There was Halma and Ludo, a chess set and draughts, Monopoly. "You need more than two people to play Monopoly," she said. She wasn't sure if she could remember how to play draughts, and chess would be too difficult for Kevin. "We could try this," she said, and pulled out a large flat box which contained a slotted peg board and boxes of coloured pegs. "This is a good game. You have to get five pegs all one colour in a straight line." It was easy to let someone else win at this game. "Let's take it down, and I'll show you. Would you carry it, please, Kevin?"

"We'll take the others too," he said, picking up the rest.

"You go first, then, as your hands are full, and I'll shut the door," said Mrs Anderson. As she did so, she turned on the light, which they had not needed on that bright afternoon with the white snow reflecting the sunshine outside. Just possibly, after dark, someone might wonder about an unusual light on the hill.

Kevin noticed nothing. As she followed him downstairs she thought it might be possible to push him down the rest of the flight to fall headlong. But he was young, and though puny, strong enough compared with herself; she might not push hard enough and he would round on her in fury.

Anyway, she could not do it: she could not physically assault this waif.

They played Five-in-a-Row for two hours. After that she taught him the same paper games that she had shown small Laura on Christmas Day.

The children's party began at three. Coaches brought the children the few miles from their institution to the hall along roads that were now cleared of snow or covered in hard, packed ice with a gritted surface. Some of the helpers travelled more perilously along country lanes. Muriel collected two other women on her way, and delivered them home again after a conjuror had entertained the children, Father Christmas had given them presents, and they had eaten a splendid tea.

"Be careful going home, Mu," said Agnes Sawyer when Muriel dropped her at Worton, a village eight miles from Framingham. "Don't go giving lifts to anyone, will you?"

"That's not very likely," said Muriel.

"I'm serious. The police are looking for that boy — the one who killed the girl from the supermarket, you remember. He's violent. He might try hitching a ride."

Muriel had not heard the broadcast about Kevin; she'd

been too busy getting things ready for the party to bother with the radio, which she rarely listened to anyway, but Agnes liked it as background noise and had heard the message.

"He wouldn't be a nice chap to meet on a dark night," Agnes warned.

Muriel had planned to go straight home. For once she wanted to be back for Howard, with the fire bright and sherry waiting. They had had such a happy time the previous day. But now she started to get out of the car.

"Mind if I use your phone, Agnes?" she asked.

"Not at all."

"I want to try to get through to an old lady I know — I tried to ring her this morning to see if she was all right in the snow, but her line's out of order. She's all on her own. She might be nervous, if she's heard about that boy."

"Ring her, of course," said Agnes.

Muriel had to look up the number in the directory. She dialled. As before, the line was dead.

"I'll go home that way and call in," Muriel said.

"Have some sherry first?"

"Love to, but better not," said Muriel. "I'd better get on."

Agnes stood in the doorway letting cold air into her centrally heated hall as Muriel climbed into the car, wool dress under sheepskin coat clinging to her.

"Go in, you'll freeze," she called, and thankfully Agnes did so. From the window she saw her friend's car disappear up the lane.

Calling at The Gables took Muriel right out of her

way; the most direct route was to go on through the lanes and Muriel did this, the car spinning a bit on the icy surface. She changed into low gear; it would have been wiser to go back along the main road, but she felt it was too late now to turn, and at last she was on the by-pass heading towards Hatch Hill.

In second gear, the car climbed steadily, and Muriel saw thick snow blocking the gateway of the house. She pulled in to the side but stopped clear of the deeper snow and got out of the car on to the icy surface of the road. She left the sidelights on, took the torch she kept in the glove compartment, and locked the car.

Two lines of footsteps marked the deep snow of the drive, going in and returning: the milk and the post, thought Muriel. Luckily she was wearing boots. She trod in the existing footsteps, picking them out with the torch.

She saw the light in the attic window as she came round the bend in the drive. Mrs Anderson never used the top floor. Uneasy, yet telling herself not to be silly, Muriel went on. The lines of footsteps went round to the back door, and Muriel followed them; Mrs Anderson's small sitting-room was nearer to there than to the front. She could see the light at the edge of the curtain across the sitting-room window, and hoped the old lady would not be alarmed when she heard someone at the door. The snow was scuffed up at the back of the house. Old people needed someone to come and clear a path for them at such a time; they had to fetch coal in, and so on. It was something that should be organized by wellwishers and Muriel made a mental note to see that in future it was someone's task to dig Mrs Anderson out in a blizzard: though with such an isolated house it was a lot to ask of a volunteer, and if Muriel had her way, Mrs Anderson would not be living at The Gables through another winter.

She pressed the back-door bell.

Kevin and Mrs Anderson both started when the bell rang shrilly through the house. They were having another game of Five-in-a-Row.

''What's that?'' Kevin sprang up, face white, eyes wide.

Mrs Anderson's heart thumped. It made a lump come into her throat and she choked a little as she answered.

''The back door,'' she said.

''Who is it?''

''I don't know,'' said Mrs Anderson.

''Are you expecting someone? Got anyone invited?''

''No.''

''How do I know you aren't lying?''

''I don't lie, Kevin.''

''You'll have to ask who's there,'' he said. ''Then say you're sick and can't see them, whoever it is.'' It couldn't be the police, they'd been already. They wouldn't come again. He caught Mrs Anderson's arm as he had that first night and twisted it behind her. Then he put a hand over her mouth. ''We're going to the door, and you're not screaming. If you do, you get it,'' he threatened. ''You ask who it is and if it's the fuzz you say you're all right and you can't open up as you've got a bad cold. Understand?'' He shook her hard.

Mrs Anderson nodded.

Kevin bundled her along the passage to the kitchen. He made her open the doors as both his hands were occupied holding on to her and covering her mouth. The bell rang again as they went from the kitchen into the rear passage, and they heard a voice.

"Mrs Anderson, can you hear me? It's Muriel Dean. I say, Mrs Anderson." The door rattled. "It's Muriel Dean," they heard again.

Kevin changed his plans. He dragged Mrs Anderson back into the kitchen, pushed her into the larder, roughly, so that she stumbled, and turned the key in the door. Then he advanced to the back door, inwardly quaking. He smoothed his hair down and stroked his embryo moustache and downy chin; then he turned off the light and opened the back door.

Muriel stepped back when she heard the bolts drawn and the door opening. She shone her torch downwards and it illumined jean-clad legs ending in grubby sneakers. Her hand shook and her actions seemed to be carried out in slow motion as she picked out the figure of a youth. He had mousy hair and was smiling. It was not a nice smile.

With a sick shock she recognized him: the boy from the garage.

"Have you come to see my grandmother?" Kevin asked, enunciating clearly. "She's in bed, I'm afraid. She's tired."

"I couldn't get through on the phone." Muriel heard a voice quite unlike her own say the words.

"It's out of order," Kevin said. In the darkness he could make out only Muriel's shape, not her features.

"She — Mrs Anderson," Muriel tried again.

"She's fine. We've been playing cards," said Kevin, still smiling. "But she's tired. Come another day," and he shut the door.

Muriel stood staring at the closed door. The boy from the garage had no business in Mrs Anderson's house masquerading as her non-existent grandson. He had to be the youth Alice had warned her about, the one wanted by the police. He'd killed that girl. What had he done to Mrs Anderson? Muriel thought of battering on the door, demanding to be let in, but if he really was a murderer he wouldn't open it. She must get the police at once.

She started down the drive towards her car.

In the house, Kevin leaned against the door, shaking. It had worked with the copper that morning; it would work with this dame, too. He turned on the light and went back into the kitchen, and opened the larder door.

Mrs Anderson lay unconscious on the cold concrete floor.

Kevin stared down at her small crumpled form. Maybe she was dead. He shut the door and locked it. Then he panicked. That one that had called, maybe she'd know that Mrs Anderson hadn't got a grandson visiting. She'd fetch the fuzz. He must stop her. He looked round for a weapon and saw none, but there was no time to waste. Just as he was, in singlet, shirt and jeans, and his canvas shoes, he ran out of the house after Muriel.

She was hurrying, but she was plump and no longer young, while Kevin was young and desperate. She did not hear him at all until he was close behind her. He flung himself at her, catching her round the hips and bringing her to the ground as he fell too. She dropped the torch and he snatched it up as she struggled in the thick, clinging snow, trying to fight him off. Kevin hit her on the head with the torch, and after that she lay still.

CHAPTER
TWENTY TWO

It was not unusual for Muriel to be out when Howard got home, but somehow he had expected to find her there tonight. The children's party must have lasted a long time, he supposed as he put a match to the fire and poured himself some sherry.

Sitting there, waiting for her, he thought about Janet with sad longing. It had to stop. If it didn't, events might develop an impetus of their own and hurtle all three of them to ruin. He looked at the leaping flames, dreaming an impossible dream of keeping both women, and therefore himself, happy, until the clock striking eight brought him back to the present.

Muriel was still out. If she'd stopped for a drink and a gossip somewhere, she would surely be home by now. He went out to the kitchen to see if there was a note for him which he'd overlooked, but there was none, nor any dinner preparations. That was very unlike Muriel; if she expected to be very late, something was left ready or there was a note telling him a steak or chops were thawing. He was quite able to cook his own meal and enjoyed it sometimes.

He felt uneasy. The roads were very treacherous and

by now even those that were clear and slushy would be icy again, for it had been freezing as he walked back from the station. Muriel was a careful driver, but in these conditions it was the other person skidding towards you that was the menace. She'd been taking some women with her to the children's party, but who? Howard hadn't been listening properly when she told him. He went to the engagement pad by the telephone and saw that she had written *Kitty and Agnes, 1.30p.m.* on today's date. He had no idea who Kitty and Agnes were. Then he remembered that Bryan Walsh had been due to perform as Father Christmas at the party. He dialled the Walshes and spoke to Betty, who had been one of the helpers. She said that Muriel had left the hall at about half-past six with Kitty Downs and Agnes Sawyer who she'd driven over.

"Why, isn't she back?" asked Betty.

"No — she's probably stopped for a drink with — er — Kitty or Agnes," said Howard. "I'll ring them. It's freezing hard and the roads will be bad."

He found Kitty's number in Muriel's book beside the telephone. He always thought of their personal telephone book as hers, since few of the numbers related to him. Kitty said that Muriel had dropped her first and then gone on to Worton with Agnes. He dialled Agnes's number. There was no reply. He went on dialling at five-minute intervals until a quarter to nine, and then he rang the police.

Kevin stood over Muriel as she lay sprawled in the snow. He shone the torch on her. Was she dead? He didn't care, but he didn't strike her again. He looked round wildly. Back in the shadows lay the house, his haven. The old woman had been right when she said that someone would come to the house in the end. Nosy busybody, he thought, looking down at the expensive sheepskin coat Muriel wore. She'd have money. He searched round for a handbag, but could not find one, so he felt for her pockets, heaving at her dead weight in the snow to move her so that he could reach them. In one, he found the keys of her car.

Kevin tossed them in the air and caught them again, grinning. A car! Of course! She'd never walk from wherever she lived. It'd mean leaving his bike and he felt a pang at that, but a car offered a better means of escape. He shone the torch towards the gate and picked his way on through the snow to where it was parked on the hill. When he unlocked it and got in, he saw Muriel's handbag on the passenger seat. It was bound to be full of money. Kevin bent to put the key in the lock. He had some trouble freeing the steering, but when he succeeded, the car started easily for it had not had time to cool completely. Kevin had never driven a car properly, but he had moved cars round Blewett's yard and he had a natural feeling for machinery. He remembered the lights, and fumbled among the switches until they came on, piercing the road ahead with a bright beam. He tried the gears. The wheels spun on the icy road and the car slithered backwards as he attempted to move off, so he stopped and tried again. This time they gripped, and rather jerkily, Kevin drove on. His spirits rose. He had a car, and loot too.

Everything would be all right now. He'd head for the north.

"Watch it, Scotland! Here I come," he said aloud.

The nearest police patrol car was sent to look for Muriel.

Police Constable Gent, the G hard as in Goat, who was teased a good deal about his name, peered out at the night, watching for an overturned car or one in the ditch as he went steadily down the winding lanes that led to the village of Worton, where the Sawyers lived. One car approached, travelling the other way, and he signalled it to stop. The driver was an elderly man who said he had met no one on his way from the village, and seen no abandoned car. Gent let him go. He carried on slowly, watching for tyre tracks running off the road into neighbouring fields where a car might lie undiscovered for hours, but there were hedges and fencing along the sides of the road for most of this area between the villages, and no signs of disturbance. His orders were to inquire at neighbours for the whereabouts of Mrs Agnes Sawyer, to see if she could explain Mrs Dean's disappearance, and if this brought no result, to drive on to Framingham, following the route probably taken by the missing woman. Meanwhile a call had gone out to stop her car, if it was seen. Middle-aged women sometimes went haywire and did strange things; driving off and vanishing into a snowy night was not totally far-fetched, though a road accident seemed the most likely explanation.

Worton lay at the foot of a winding hill, a straggling village gathered round a church, with two pubs and a couple of shops, one of which doubled as a post office. There was a sparse bus service. Most of the residents were commuters who drove to Framingham station and in the week the village was dead in the day-time. Agnes, when she wanted the car, took her husband to the station and met him again in the evening.

Gent asked at the Pig and Whistle for directions to the Sawyers' house, and was told it was two hundred yards down the road on the left. He returned to his car and drove on, leaving the company in the bar wondering what the police wanted with the respectable Sawyers.

Gent stopped by their gate and walked up the short drive to the front door. The snow had been cleared from the path, fairy lights shone from an artificial Christmas tree in the hall window, and the porch light was on. No one answered when Gent rang the bell. He went round to the rear of the house and tried the back door, then shone his torch on the window of the garage. A blue Audi was inside.

Gent tried the houses on either side of the Sawyers' but they were empty too, and the cars were in the garages. He went on up the road and after finding four houses in a row deserted but for a yapping dog in one of them, went back to fetch his car. He rang in to say that he was trying other houses further along the road. The entire population of the village couldn't have vanished, leaving their cars at home; they must be at a party or in the bar of the other pub, the Grinning Monkey. In patches, the footpath by the side of the road had been swept, but for great stretches it lay covered in snow pitted with footmarks, and Gent found the party by tracking them to the Manor House, which lay down a side road where there were only a few tyre marks in the snow, and the footprints of about twenty people. Hoping he would be able to drive out again, he went along the lane. In one spot there was a cleared area where someone had dug out a drift. He drove on and came to a gateway set between high stone walls. The tyre marks emerged from here, and a path had been cut through the snow. Gent left his car at the gate and got out. He saw a large, graceful, Queen Anne house at the end of a carriage sweep. Lights shone from every window.

He found Agnes Sawyer, with many of the other residents of Worton, carrying on Christmas in the depths of the snowbound countryside.

Muriel's face was pressed into the snow; it trickled wetly down her neck. She felt very cold. She lay there, trying to recollect what had happened, conscious of a thumping headache. After a little while she struggled to her feet. Her limbs seemed to work. The soft snow had cushioned her fall, and her thick coat, her boots and her sheepskin gloves had protected her from the worst of the cold.

Round her, trees sighed in a light wind; the night was dark but the sky was clear and starlit. Muriel knew she had to do something important, there was no time to lose. At last she remembered about Mrs Anderson and the boy. She looked round for her torch, stooping and fumbling about in the snow for it, but could not find it, so she set off towards the car without it. The police. She must fetch the police.

Muriel's progress to the gate followed a zigzag course, brains and limbs lacking coordination. When she got there, there was no car. But surely she had come by car? She gazed round at the night. This must be Hatch Hill. She patted her pocket, where she would normally put her keys if she had no handbag with her, but there was no familiar bulge. She took off her gloves and felt in both pockets. No keys. Perhaps she had had her bag with her, then? She was very confused, but she knew she had to fetch the police urgently. It came to her that she was here because Mrs Anderson's telephone was out of order. She was too disoriented at first to realize that the boy must have taken her car, but at last she worked it out. What should she do? Should she walk to the nearest house or telephone box, or return up the drive and try to get in to The Gables, to see what had happened to Mrs Anderson?

The decision seemed impossibly difficult.

Howard leaped to answer the telephone when it rang. As he expected, hoped and dreaded, it was the police, but they had not found Muriel. A voice asked if Howard knew the identity of an old lady living alone about whom his wife was concerned and whom she might have gone to see on her way home from the village of Worton.

Howard knew that all right. Hatch Hill wasn't exactly on the way home, but Muriel had been uneasy when she couldn't get through to Mrs Anderson on the telephone. He told the constable, and his own concern turned to irritation. Muriel must be chatting to the old lady, forgetting the time. She should realize he would be anxious, in such weather. Of course, with Mrs Anderson's telephone not working, she couldn't let him know where she was. She might have got stuck with the car on Hatch Hill. He tried to temper his annoyance with sweet reason but didn't get very far. Muriel's involvement with other people's welfare was exceedingly trying.

He thought of walking to Hatch Hill to see if she was marooned, but then decided not to. The police would get there long before he could, and if Muriel was in a snowdrift, she would be tired, hungry, and in need of a drink when she was rescued.

He went out to the kitchen to start rustling up some supper.

Muriel blundered along the drive, stumbling in the snow, trying to follow the tracks already there, but without a torch it was difficult to see them. Distance was deceptive, and at times she floundered in deep snow, then in other spots found the ground firm, barely covered. In spite of her thick coat, she was shivering, her teeth chattering and her whole body trembling. She came towards the house at last and saw a shaft of light fanning out from the back door which Kevin had left open in his flight. Muriel managed to put on some speed at this sight and soon she was on the step, where she had rung the bell — how long before? She did not know if it had been hours or merely minutes.

The door from the kitchen into the passage was ajar. Muriel pushed it open and went in, calling, ''Mrs

Anderson? Mrs Anderson? Are you all right?''

The room was empty.

Muriel hurried through it into the hall and then to Mrs Anderson's sitting-room. The light was on here, too. On the table, laid out for play by two people, was a game Muriel had played with her own children, Five-in-a-Row. The paraffin stove was out and the room was chilly. There was no one there.

Muriel set off to search the rest of the house. She would try the attic first, where, as she now remembered, she had seen that warning light.

Driving the Maxi was very different from riding his motorbike. Kevin had enough road sense to be careful with the brake, but even so he slithered and skidded trying to slow down to see a signpost two miles beyond The Gables. He did not know which was the road to the north, but decided to keep going straight ahead, where the sign pointed to Dartworth. White and hard under the tyres, the packed snow had turned to ice and stretched brilliantly ahead of him in the lights of the car. If he kept on he would meet a main road at last and then he could really travel.

Warmth came from the car's heater, left on by Muriel, so that Kevin forgot he had no coat and that his feet were in soaking canvas shoes. The driving seat was too far back for him but he did not stop to adjust it.

Settling to the feel of the car, Kevin fiddled with the different controls. He found the screenwashers, but they were frozen up and emitted only a whine. His searching hand met, eventually, the radio. Great! He'd never thought of that; what a way to live, driving a car like this with a radio fitted! He pressed various buttons and located his pop programme.

He came to a main road intersection at last; it stretched wide and black away from him, clear of snow but with slush hardening into ridges at the sides. Kevin swung out, turning left, where the sign pointed to the M1. That went north, didn't it? He could go faster now. He put his foot down, gripping the steering-wheel, leaning forward, concentrating. He was happy.

Muriel opened the door of the attic room that lay to her left. Inside, lit by the solitary bulb under a plain glass shade on a flex in the centre of the room, she saw a large cupboard which, when opened, revealed toys: trains and model cars, lead soldiers and farm animals.

Mrs Anderson was not in the room. Muriel closed the door, leaving the light on, and tried the other two rooms on the landing. The middle one had clearly once been a maid's bedroom: the narrow bed and austere furnishing were typical of accommodation provided by an employer thirty-five or more years ago.

In the third room she saw a shirt on a wire hanger, leather boots in a corner, a leather jacket on the back of a chair. A transistor radio was on the bedside table, with a cup and saucer, plate and knife beside it. An electric fire was on and the room was very warm; it had a faint, indefinable smell: a personal smell. Muriel could not work out the implications now; she was concerned only with finding Mrs Anderson. She might be locked up somewhere, a prisoner, murdered.

Not afraid, because if the youth had taken off in her car he could not attack her again, Muriel concentrated on searching for the old lady. She tried every room, and every cupboard in every room. She looked under beds and in the linen cupboard, and the housemaid's cupboard on the first landing. She searched Mrs Anderson's own room with its large, heavy furniture crammed into a small space, and the other, sheeted bedrooms.

Downstairs, she examined the drawing-room, the dining-room, the study, and a large cupboard under the stairs. She went into the cloakroom and saw on pegs the cap and old raincoat that Kevin had worn that morning when Police Constable Frewen called at the house. A small pool of water had collected on the floor beside a pair of boots.

Muriel went through the kitchen again and into the rear passage. She looked in the bootroom and saw, with puzzled astonishment, the burnt fur stole in its pail. She went into the pantry and down to the musty cellar where cobwebs clung to the corners, and two rusted bicycles hung from hooks on the wall. Some bowls containing bulb fibre, with white spikes of shoots just visible, stood on a shelf beside two bottles of claret which lay on their sides in an otherwise empty rack.

There was no trace of the old lady.

She would have to search the outbuildings. There were sheds and the garage. How could she do it, without a torch? Muriel looked in the hall, which was where she and Howard always kept one, but Mrs Anderson did not seem to do the same sensible thing. Muriel tried

233

cupboards and drawers. She went to the desk in the sitting-room, and she discovered the returned letters, but she found no torch.

There were matches, though, on the mantelpiece, used for the paraffin heater.

Crossing the kitchen again, on her way to the outbuildings, Muriel looked at the closed larder door.

CHAPTER
TWENTY THREE

Muriel met Police Constable Gent at the gate. She heard her own voice break and her remarks, meant to be sensible, turning to sobs as she collapsed against the constable's sturdy form.

Gent picked out one or two words. ''She's going to die — you must help her — back in the house — '' Muriel wailed. ''She's so old — she's sure to die.''

Gent, one arm round her, spoke into his radio, giving a preliminary message.

''Can you show me? It'll save time,'' he said. ''Now come along, madam.'' His voice was sharp and it gave Muriel the spur she needed to regain control.

''Yes — back there — he was here, that boy — '' Muriel's voice steadied. ''That boy you want. The boy from the garage.''

''He's gone?''

''He's taken my car,'' said Muriel, clinging to the constable's arm.

Gent radioed in, asking for help and reporting what she had said. Then, with his arm supporting her, the two of them trudged to the house. To Muriel, making the journey for the third time that evening, it seemed a distance of twenty miles as her leaden legs carried her reluctantly along, Gent's powerful torch lighting the way.

Somehow she had found the strength to move Mrs Anderson to the kitchen, where it was warm, for she had been icy to the touch. Even if limbs were broken, left where she was while Muriel went for help she would die of exposure if she were not, in fact, already dead. Muriel thought she could detect a thread-like pulse, but she was so cold and shaky herself that she could not be sure. She had laid the old woman on the mat in front of the Aga, then gone upstairs for blankets and a pillow, and wrapped her up, cocooning her like a baby. She'd found a hot-water bottle and filled it, tucking it in with her before setting off.

Gent bent over Mrs Anderson where she lay exactly as Muriel had left her.

"She's breathing," he said, and gave Muriel a smile. "Sit down, Mrs Dean. Help will soon be here now."

Muriel subsided on to a chair by the table. She scarcely heard as the constable spoke into his radio. Very quickly indeed, another police constable and a woman police constable arrived; then the ambulance. Muriel heard snatches of talk between the officers but she did not try to understand. She was shivering again, and she went on shivering when she was in the ambulance with Mrs Anderson, who was ashen-faced and almost invisible under the grey blankets.

Kevin ran out of petrol on the M1 just south of Leicester. Till then, he had been driving at a steady speed, adjusted to the rhythm of the car and, in top gear, not required to do much more than maintain speed and to steer. He thought of nothing but the car, enjoying its power and comfort as he sat, warm and dry, moving through the night. As he went further north where more snow had fallen, only one lane of the motorway was clear so that he was forced to slow down and proceed head to tail in convoy with other traffic. The car juddered in top gear but he changed down smoothly; then, after a few more miles, it began to misfire, jerking and hesitating, until finally the engine stopped altogether and the speed fell right away. The car behind blasted its horn as the Maxi seemed to fall back towards it. Kevin retained enough sense, seeing the lights behind him in the mirror, to steer off the highway towards the shoulder, but the swept snow made a barrier and the car stopped almost at once, barely out of the way of the following traffic. He tried the starter again and again, but nothing happened. After a time he thought of looking at the petrol gauge and saw the needle registering empty. He cursed then, swearing at the car, the woman he'd stolen it from who hadn't filled the tank, the weather, everything but himself.

Traffic passed him, sending splutters of slush against the car as he sat there clasping the wheel and shouting obscenities while pop still blared forth from the radio.

He'd get a lift. He couldn't stay here.

Kevin opened the driver's door and immediately horns blared at him as traffic swerved away. Slush spurted against him and his sneakers were soaked. The cold wind struck him like a whip.

Cars and lorries lumbered by, drenching him and missing him by inches. He went round to the rear of the

Maxi and signalled with his thumb, but no one stopped for him.

After a while Kevin began walking, hands thrust into the pockets of his jeans, thin body protected from the bitter weather only by singlet and shirt. In the falling snow his slight figure was scarcely visible, stumbling along in the slush. At intervals he turned in the glare of the headlights and stuck up his thumb in the hitch-hiker's universal gesture. The driver of the big container lorry, its cab high above the road, did not see him until he was almost on top of him. He swerved, but there was a thud as Kevin's body was struck and thrown into the snow at the side of the highway.

A uniformed officer came to tell Howard that Muriel had been found and was on her way to Allington General Hospital. Howard received a severe shock at the news. The policeman took him to the hospital but could tell him very little about what had happened, though it seemed that in addition to somehow getting hurt, Muriel had allowed the Maxi to be stolen.

She had been X-rayed and was already in bed in a small ward when Howard reached the hospital. Neither spoke as he kissed her gently and then held her hand. There was pallor behind the thread-like veins on her face, and she looked exhausted. Howard supposed that someone would eventually tell him what had happened to cause her to lie unconscious in the snow for over two hours.

"I'm all right — I've just got a bump on my head," Muriel said. "I'll be home tomorrow. I don't know why

I can't come now," and she began to tremble, then to weep. Large tears flowed from her eyes, a sight Howard had almost never seen. "Mrs Anderson — " Muriel wept harder, unable to say anything about Mrs Anderson.

"Don't try to talk," advised Howard. "It'll keep till you feel better."

"She may die," Muriel managed to wail.

"I'm sure she'll be all right," said Howard, who did not care about Mrs Anderson, the cause in some way of Muriel's downfall.

"Don't tell the girls," Muriel sniffed. "Not till I'm home again. They'd only worry. And Felicity's in Austria by now."

Howard promised not to alarm their daughters.

"The police were so kind," said Muriel, her sobs decreasing. "It was clever of them to know Kevin Timms was up there. That must have been why they came to The Gables."

"They were looking for you," said Howard. Who was Kevin Timms? He recalled something he had heard people discussing on the train, and his bewilderment grew. Did Kevin Timms, wanted for murder, come into this somewhere? He pressed on. "You were late home, and I was worried. Luckily you'd told Agnes Sawyer where you were going."

"Oh — is that what happened? I thought it was the police," said Muriel. The sedative she had been given was beginning to work now and she spoke drowsily. "Do you know, Howard, suddenly I'm too sleepy to come home tonight anyway."

"You rest, then. I'm sure they'll let you out in the morning," said Howard.

"Persuade them, won't you?" Muriel said. "I'm glad you missed me, Howard," and she closed her eyes.

"He ate them," mumbled Mrs Anderson. "It wasn't me. I didn't do it." She stirred in the high bed.

The nurse taking her pulse said soothingly, "There, there, everything's all right."

"The money too. I'm not mad," said Mrs Anderson. She opened her eyes and shot a blue glance up at the young girl.

"No dear, of course you're not. What an idea," said the nurse.

"Beans. Eggs. All that butter," Mrs Anderson went on. "And the bread, cutting it like that."

"Yes, dear. Never mind about it now."

"And the blue scarf Helen gave me."

The nurse patted her hand and went to tell sister that Mrs Anderson was delirious.

CHAPTER
TWENTY FOUR

Howard spent a near-sleepless night. Before he left the hospital, a policeman had come to take a statement from Muriel, but finding her very drowsy, and discouraged sternly by the sister, had asked a few questions and decided to leave the rest until the morning. Howard, knowing only the bare outline of what had happened, tortured himself imagining a figure stealing up behind his wife and hitting her on the head. Had the blow been harder, or in a different spot, she might have died.

He telephoned the office to say that he would not be coming in that day, and then Agnes Sawyer called him, offering to drive him to the hospital, to collect Muriel or to visit her, whichever was appropriate. She had rung the night before during the hours when Muriel was missing, asking to be told as soon as there was news, and Howard had telephoned her from the hospital. Her husband had immediately come over in his blue Audi to drive Howard home. Such kindness was overwhelming to Howard, who had met neither of the Sawyers before, and, indeed, had barely heard of them. If Agnes had not known where Muriel was going, she might have collapsed as she went for help and lain for hours undiscovered in the snow. But the worst thought of all was that some boy already guilty of one killing had tried to murder her.

While Howard waited for Agnes, the police telephoned to say that the Maxi had been found the night before abandoned on the M1 near Leicester, with the lights full on. It seemed to be undamaged, and Muriel's handbag was on the seat, apparently untouched.

It was snowing lightly when Agnes arrived, and she drove cautiously to Allington, sitting forward in her seat and peering past the wipers.

"Poor Mu — what a terrible experience," she said. "If that old lady survives, it will be thanks to her. The police didn't know Kevin Timms was hiding up there, did they?"

It seemed clear that they had not.

When they reached the hospital, Muriel was not to be seen, but the sister said she had slept well, the X-rays had shown no fracture, and she was now visiting Mrs Anderson who was in a side ward on her own.

Howard and Agnes exchanged glances.

"It's all right," said Agnes. "She's back on form."

They waited for her, sitting on a hard leather bench in the passage, and after ten minutes saw her coming towards them, more slowly than usual, perhaps, and a little pale, but smiling.

"Poor Mrs Anderson," she said. "The nurses thought she was raving because she kept talking about someone eating things. She meant that boy. He must have been in the house for days and helped himself to her stores. He hid from her somehow, she told me. I don't think she really knows the details. Oh Howard, do you think he was there on Christmas Day, and we never realized? How dreadful! One of those attic rooms looked as if it had been occupied for a while.''

''It's no good worrying about that now, darling,'' said Howard. ''I expect the police will be able to tell you all about it in due time.''

''Have they caught him yet?''

''Not as far as I know, but they've found the car.'' Howard told her about it, and about her handbag.

''It's the one you gave me for Christmas. I'd have hated to lose it,'' said Muriel. ''But he must have panicked or he'd have taken the money from it. They'll soon catch him now.''

They heard about Kevin later that morning when a woman police constable called at Beech House to take a detailed statement from Muriel. There had been a pile-up on the motorway after the container lorry which struck Kevin had jack-knifed when it skidded to a halt. Several people had been badly hurt in the resulting chaos, and the facts about what had happened had not been clear at first. When the police established the ownership of the Maxi found abandoned half a mile from the scene of the accident, they knew that Kevin Timms was in the area, but by then ambulances were on their way to collect the injured. Weather conditions were bad; the youth lying in the snow had no papers on him to show who he was, and it had taken a little time for the police to realize that their hunt was over. By then the fugutive was in the casualty department of the nearest hospital, but he was not badly hurt: a broken arm and concussion, said the police officer.

Muriel digested this information.

"If Mrs Anderson dies, he'll have murdered her," she said.

"No," said Howard. "Not unless he'd directly attacked her. Had he?"

She'd insisted not, Muriel said, although he'd certainly locked her in the larder.

Howard was allowed to remain while she told her story to the police. He listened quietly. There would be plenty of evidence to prove Kevin had broken into The Gables and slept there, but that alone would not earn him a heavy sentence. He would go down on what he had done to the girl. A good counsel might get him off a murder rap, and if he were convicted of manslaughter he might not be out of circulation long.

Sprockett called to tell Jessie that Kevin was in hospital. He would be charged with various offences when he was well enough to be brought back to Allington.

"Has he been with friends?" There might be someone — someone besides herself — who cared for him.

It would be in the paper the next day. Sprockett had prepared the statement for the press himself.

"He'd been hiding up at a house outside Framingham," said Sprockett. They'd found his motor-bike in the garden shed at The Gables.

"Did he — did he hurt anyone else?"

Sprockett decided not to mention Mrs Dean. She'd learn it all soon enough.

"An old lady was concerned. The householder," he said. "She isn't well enough yet to be questioned."

244

"Then he did hurt her."

"Well, she's very old, and she was alone with him in the blizzard," said Sprockett.

There was no need to mention Kevin Timms' attempt to pass himself off as her grandson, duly entered in Police Constable Frewen's report. Sprockett intended to see the constable about that episode without delay.

"Poor Kevin. Maybe if he pays for what he's done, he'll learn better ways," said Jessie, sighing. "I'll go and see him. May I?"

Sprockett said that it would be better to wait for a while. She could write to him, if she wished. He knew that Kevin, in his present mood, would be abusive to his aunt. Whatever happened, he was only nineteen and would have years ahead of him when he came out of gaol where he would make contacts with others like himself. Sprockett thought the chances of Timms becoming a worthwhile citizen were small indeed.

When Sprockett had gone, Jessie sat staring into space wondering what she could have done to make things work out differently for Kevin. She'd saved him once from the consequences of his actions; she could do nothing, now, to help him.

She was still sitting there when Bob came.

Laura had to be told a little about what had happened, since it was reported in the press and would be talked about for days in the locality. Through Emily, Janet learned how Muriel was; for some reason she did not understand, she could not bring herself to telephone direct. The papers described

Mrs Anderson's condition as serious.

Laura knew that you took flowers to ill people. She consulted Jenny's mother about how it could be done on Friday morning, disclosing the amount available in her piggy bank. Jenny's mother was sympathetic and helpful; her husband, an accountant, worked in Allington and would take a posy to Mrs Anderson, now admitted by Jenny not to be a witch after all, at the hospital next week. Laura herself could deliver one to Muriel. Jenny's mother would lend her the money so that she could do it right away.

By silent agreement, neither child mentioned their foray into the garden of The Gables. They did not know that Kevin Timms had been in there at the time.

That afternoon, a bunch of anemones in her hand, Laura stood on the doorstep of Beech House, ringing the bell.

The door was opened by Mrs Wilson, who expected to see an importunate journalist. Howard had instructed, when he went to the station that morning leaving Mrs Wilson looking after Muriel, that all reporters were to be sent away, and Mrs Wilson adopted a belligerent stance, standing athwart the doorway as she opened the door.

"I came to see Mrs Dean," said Laura.

"She can't see anyone," said Mrs Wilson. "She isn't well." She muted her aggression slightly, to suit the size of the caller.

"I know. That's why I've come," said Laura firmly. "To visit the sick."

"Who is it, Mrs Wilson?" Muriel called. She had

spent a boring day, though glad to have breakfast in bed and her lunch prepared. She had surprised herself by being unable to sleep without the pill Dr Baynes, whom Howard had insisted should see her after she returned from hospital, had left for her, and was dismayed at feeling weak today. It was unnatural to her, though, to sit still, and she couldn't settle to a book. "Who's there?" she repeated.

Mrs Wilson surrendered.

"Who shall I say?" she asked. "What's your name?"

Laura told her, and Mrs Wilson beckoned her into the hall, closing the front door. She led the way to the sitting-room and held the door for Laura to enter.

"Laura Finch," Mrs Wilson announced formally.

"Laura, what a nice surprise," said Muriel, holding out a hand as the child entered. "Mrs Wilson, I'm sure Laura would like some orange squash. Or a Coca-Cola. Which would you like, Laura?"

Laura chose orange, and Muriel told her to take off her coat and sit down.

"You'd better take those wet boots off too," said Mrs Wilson, and when Laura had done so, bore them off to lay them on newspaper in the cloakroom.

Laura then advanced towards Muriel with her flowers.

"How lovely. Thank you," said Muriel.

"I hope you'll soon be better," Laura said.

"I'm quite all right. I've just got to rest for a day or two," said Muriel.

"How's Mrs Anderson?" Laura asked.

"Well — she's rather old," said Muriel. "It may take a little longer for her to get better."

Mrs Wilson came in then with a glass of orange squash and a plate with two chocolate biscuits on it, on a tray. She set it down in front of Laura, who nibbled the biscuits in a dainty manner she thought appropriate to the occasion. Muriel wondered how to entertain her, since she seemed to be settling down.

They were playing Spillikins when Mrs Wilson came in to say that she was leaving. She'd left a tea tray ready, and Mr Dean had said he'd be home early.

"Mummy said he might not come to see us tonight," Laura said, carefully pulling a spillikin from the pile of sticks.

Neither Muriel nor Mrs Wilson spoke. Laura detached another spillikin and looked at them. They were both staring at her dumbfounded.

"He always has supper with us on Friday," she explained, since they seemed surprised. "Sometimes he brings me a present."

Mrs Wilson recovered first.

"Time you went home, young lady," she said. "Your mother will be wondering where you are. Come along, your things are in the cloakroom."

She swept the child ahead of her out of the room.

Half an hour later, when Howard came home, Muriel was sitting, oddly idle, by the fire. It struck him that he seldom saw her in total repose, and her hands were tensely clasped now.

Mrs Wilson had overheard Laura's revelation; she had not missed its meaning, though she had not mentioned it when she returned to Muriel after the child had gone. She had made up the fire, plumped up the cushions behind Muriel and delayed long enough to make tea for her before at last departing.

Muriel accepted Howard's kiss on her cheek. She wondered how she was going to manage the next minutes, indeed, how she would manage the rest of her life. She might attempt to ignore what Laura had said, but at this moment it seemed to her that her whole marriage must have been a lie.

Mrs Anderson was propped up in bed. She felt very weak and rather as if she were floating in some area near the ceiling. Beside her were Detective Chief Inspector Sprockett and a woman police constable. They had managed to persuade sister into letting them talk to her for ten minutes.

"We played cards," she said. "He was just a poor, silly boy. He didn't hurt me." She remembered the blows and decided she would not mention them. "He was frightened," she added.

There was a large bruise on her face, yellowing now. She could have got it falling to the larder floor. Her arm, protruding from the hospital nightgown, was bruised too.

"I expect he thought it was rather a large house for one old lady to live in alone," Mrs Anderson said, the words coming slowly because she was a little breathless. "He was right."

"Had he stolen anything? Did you miss anything?"

"Nothing of value. A few tins of food," said Mrs Anderson.

"He locked you in. Are you sure he didn't attack

you?'' Sprockett asked.

''No, inspector. We played games together. I told you,'' said Mrs Anderson.

Sprockett saw that he would not be able to get her to say anything that would enable him to charge Timms with assaulting her. Maybe she would change her mind later, if she recovered.

''Will you see that the boy has a pack of cards in — in prison?'' said Mrs Anderson. ''I taught him to play patience. I will give you the money later. I'm afraid I have none here with me at present.''

''I'll attend to it, Mrs Anderson,'' said Sprockett.

Muriel Dean would see about money, Mrs Anderson thought: find her handbag, cash cheques for her personal needs while she was in hospital. Was she going to recover? She was still alive, so she probably would, but what sort of future could there be for her if she did? She would never be able to live alone in that house again.

Muriel would help her: Muriel would know what to do.

The publishers hope that this large print book has brought you pleasurable reading. Each title is designed to make the text as easy to read as possible.

For further information on backlist or forthcoming titles please write or telephone:

In the British Isles and its territories, customers should contact:

ISIS Publishing Ltd
7 Centremead
Osney Mead
Oxford OX2 0ES
England
Telephone: (01865) 250 333 Fax: (01865) 790 358

In Australia and New Zealand, customers should contact:

Bolinda Publishing Pty Ltd
17 Mohr Street
Tullamarine Victoria 3043
Australia
Telephone: (03) 9338 0666 Fax: (03) 9335 1903
Toll Free Telephone: 1800 335 364
Toll Free Fax: 1800 671 4111

In New Zealand:
Toll Free Telephone: 0800 44 5788
Toll Free Fax: 0800 44 5789